Witching Moon
Twisted Dark

Anna M.L. Koski

ISBN-13: 978-1775185703
ISBN-10: 1775185702

WITCHING MOON

Copyright © 2017 by Anna M. L. Koski

All rights reserved, including the right of reproduction in whole or part form.

This book is a work of fiction and any reference to real historical events, people, locations are used fictitiously. Other names, characters, places, and incidents are the product of the author's imagination and any resemblance to actual events or places or persons, living or dead, is purely coincidental.

Also available in eBook with Amazon.

Cover Image by Alex Powell (Pexels), Alexander Krivitskiy (Pexels)

Cover Design by *The Round Table*

To my sisters
For always being there for me

Curse of the Stone Hearted Witch

In darkness I cast
In the shadows I hide
The dark gods I ask
Punish he who has lied

Make him feel
The heart he broke
Teach him to heel
Under a heavy yoke

Remove what he craves
As he left me to lie
His behaviour depraved
While our child has died

Punish not one
Punish them all
Let the curse be done
Let the Werewolves fall

~

Rowenya Stoneheart
Level Seven Elder Witch
Spurned lover of Ragnor the Great
Curser of the Werewolf species

Ballad of BamBam

Remove their futures
Remove their guides
Let them flounder
With their pride

Punish those who seek
And those who lie
You fuck with me bitch
You're in for a ride

~

BamBam
Level Seven Witch
Breaker of rules
Lover of the depraved
BANISHED

Chapter One
Witches and Weres

My truck sputtered, warning me of its immanent demise and I narrowed my eyes at it as I slammed my hand against the steering wheel. "If you fucking die on me right now I am going to be *so* pissed!" The engine sputtered and I narrowed my eyes. Not this fucking time, not when it was fucking raining out. I pressed my hand to the dash and chanted a few short, clipped words and runes glowed on my skin as they sunk into the metal dashboard under my palm. The truck sputtered and then roared its acceptance of the magick.

I gave a smug smirk as I pulled it off of the shoulder of the road and back onto the highway. They could take all my hard earned gold and fucking banish me to the outer realms of the Territory with nothing but a shitty little cabin and an ancient truck but they couldn't take the magick that ran through my veins. I was a witch.

2

I was born a witch.

I lived as a witch.

I would die as a witch.

Sure, I bent the rules, as per why I was banished to begin with, but they were always so stuffy and they all looked like they had sticks shoved up their asses. It wasn't *my* fault I had been banished. If that stupid and naive witch hadn't decided to go after me because I just happened to have fucked her little warlock, emphasis on the little, I wouldn't have been in this position at all.

I didn't even know why she was upset, he wasn't even a good lay, fucking terrible to be honest, especially with his pencil dick. He was seriously disappointing. If anything she should have gone after *him.* After sleeping with him I could understand she probably had a lot of internal aggression that caused her to lash out due to the fact she was completely and totally sexually unfulfilled. The guy couldn't satisfy anyone with his gear, not that he had even tried. Stupidity on his part but it came with that stupid *'not enough warlocks to go around'* bullshit we lived with. If he had decided to pay even the *least* bit of attention to his partner's needs then I doubted I would have exploded her when she tried to curse me.

I scowled darkly, they hadn't even banished me for exploding the witch. It was something that happened all the time, magick tended to be volatile at times. No, they fucking banished me because of how I did it.

Magick is to be used with purified tools and within the organized structures set out by the Elders.

One of the big fucking rules and I broke it because I just happened to use my magick with an

3

'*unpurified tool that resulted in a highly volatile spell which killed a fellow witch.*'. If I wouldn't have been so offended they called my body impure I would have tried to argue that the volatility of my spell had been deliberate and I had *wanted* to turn the witch into paste.

I let out an irritated breath. What was done was done and I couldn't change it. I had my cabin, as pathetic as it was at times, my truck, as shitty and ancient as it was. I had food and clothing but I was still unsatisfied. I was running an unfortunate, totally unwanted, dry spell. I hadn't had sex in *months*. It was fucking grating.

I stared out into the dark, cursing the flickering headlights in the not so clear night. I couldn't keep using magick to keep the rattle trap going. I knew it would give out eventually. It let out another rattling whine and I gave it another surge of magick. I needed it to make it back to the cabin, once I was back there I could try and con someone into looking at it and perhaps fixing it. I wasn't completely useless or without some skills other than magick.

Something appeared on the road as my lights flickered and I let out a curse and yanked the wheel to the side to avoid it. More curses tumbled out of my mouth as the truck skidded on the slick surface of the road and tilted on two wheels. A frustrated shout left my mouth as I pressed my hands to the body of the truck and quickly spat out a spell. The runes on my skin glowed sharply and the truck left the ground, the magick absorbing the momentum and allowing the truck to land safely on all of its wheels.

Once the truck landed I yanked off my seat belt, anger seething inside of me. Of all the stupid and idiotic things! I shoved open the door and it screeched into the rainy night as I stalked towards whatever it was that had nearly ruined my night entirely. The rain was coming down heavier than I expected and I held out my hands, the runes glowing on my skin. My palms lit up, flames dancing between my fingers as the glow of them illuminated the area.

I moved forward, catching sight of a gleam through the darkness and rain. A tall figure cast a faint shadowy form and I narrowed my eyes at it. "What's your fucking deal? Walking down the middle of the highway in the rain. Are you *stupid*?" A deep and guttural growl was all I got in response and my scowl darkened.

A fucking werewolf, just my luck.

I stormed closer, letting my anger fuel the fire warming my hands, creating a bigger glow. "Listen here you big wolf, piece of shit. I nearly crashed my truck because of you!" I was perfectly content exploding him into millions of itty bitty pieces. I stayed away from the werewolves because they didn't fuck with my turf. This douche rocket was ruining my perfectly crafted system of don't fuck with me and I won't fuck with you.

Eyes gleamed at me, narrowing as a deep growl vibrated from the form. I ignored his agitation as I stalked towards him, the glow from the flames was making him more visible. I hesitated for a brief moment, the dude was fucking cut. His wet shirt clung to his perfectly sculpted form like a second skin and a rush of heat moved through me. His body was more than fuckable, it was down right worship-able. My lips parted and I felt the warm rush of arousal sing through my veins.

The flames in my hand flickered and without warning he leapt towards me. He grabbed my wrists tightly with one hand, snuffing out the flames as he twisted me around, pulling me close as his teeth scrapped my neck in warning. I shuddered against him. I had been without a male companion in months and werewolf or not, this male was *prime*. I nearly groaned as his hot breath brushed across my wet skin.

"Witchling." It was a garbled word and my knees felt weak as the low, rough and sinuous quality his voice had. I wondered what he would do if I dropped to my knees to worship him properly.

A giggle formed in my throat and I fought really hard to hold it back. It wouldn't be proper to giggle in such a situation. I didn't even attempt to fight how my body instinctively pressed closer to his. I shivered at the contact of his hard planes of muscles against me. I inhaled deeply, smelling the wild, animalistic scent of the wolf on him, and I shivered at it. A rather dangerous thought formed in my head.

I had never had a Were before.

I sucked my bottom lip into my mouth as his grip grew tighter, pulling me closer. "*Witchling.*" There was a distinct warning to the growled word and I felt a small pout form as I slowly let my bottom lip slip out from between my teeth. If he tried to harm me I would have to kill him and it would be such a waste of prime male flesh to do so.

"Were." I fairly purred the word at him, unable to help myself. "It seems we are at an impasse. You have my hands and we all know witches cannot do magick without them." Only *boring* witches couldn't do magic without their hands, only witches who followed the *rules* couldn't do magick without their hands. I was more than perfectly capable of doing magick without them. It helped when my body was the only tool I used for casting and I certainly didn't need hands to utilize it.

His teeth scraped against my neck and I could feel goosebumps following the dangerously sharp points of his canines. "Kill you now?" He seemed to grin, as if liking the position we were in. I frowned slightly, that was no good. I didn't like males who lorded over me.

With one swift move I shoved hard against him, he gave a chuckle as if amused at my pathetic escape attempt. I grinned as I tilted my head to the side, he drew his nose across the pale column, as if liking the invitation I had given him. I let my hands go limp in his grasp, giving the slight illusion of surrender as chanted silently under my breath.

I could feel my body heating as the specific runes glowed on my skin. My skin heated slowly until I could see it glowing. The werewolf gave a sharp growl and shoved me away as his skin burned against my own. I whirled around, my eyes on him as the water on me steamed and then evaporated against my super heated skin. One of my best defensive spells I had. Some males didn't know what no meant.

His eyes glowed in the dark and made a show of stretching my arms above my head, his gaze trailed down my body in a way that seemed distinctly appreciative. I quirked an eyebrow at it as I made a mental note that weremales were in fact highly instinctive and followed the three basic instincts.

Fight, feed, and breed.

I couldn't help the delightful shiver I got at the thought of it. I wondered if he would be willing to cross that inter-species line. I knew I was fully on board with the idea, especially with him looking like *that*.

"Seems you lost your advantage, Were. Pity. I was quite enjoying it." I did miss his body pressed against mine, I was left shivering slightly at he loss of his hard and heated body pressed against mine. I had been denied sex for far too long, which was a terrible thing for someone who was used to getting it at least twice a week and those were the *bad* weeks. "I have no quarrel with you. I was just upset about my truck." I looked him over and realized he had slowly started circling me, his nose raised slightly as if he were scenting the air.

"Bapa?" At the childish voice my head snapped to the side.

A child!

He let out a deafening snarl that I ignored as my own instinct drove me to seek it out. If witches had one weakness it was children. Or perhaps it was just me. I adored the little rugrats, felt a bone deep need to touch them whenever I saw them.

I saw a tiny huddled form hiding at the edge of the road and turned my head just in time to throw out a hand and send the weremale flying across the road and into the trees on the other side.

Babies came first.

"Hey little one. Come on out." I crouched down and held my arms out, my fingers gesturing to the little soaked creature. Eyes gleamed at me and I knew it was a werewolf but that mattered little to me. A child was a child and I needed to touch. "Come, come. I won't hurt you." I tucked my wet hair behind my ears as I sat down on the wet asphalt. I reached out again and the tiny figure moved closer, its gleaming eyes darting to where the male was growling and snarling in the trees.

"Come, baby. Come here." I reached out further. I needed to touch, it was a bone deep compulsion. I loved children. They were like my goddamned Achilles' heel. The tiny form moved closer and stretched out a hand hesitantly. "That's it, sweet one, come on." I reached out and a loud horn shattered the still pitter patter of the falling rain scaring the child back into the darkness of the ditch. I frowned as I watched it scurry off before, without warning, I was thrown in after it.

Chapter Two
Manipulating Instinct

Protect

The action was instinctive as we wrapped our hands around the female and tossed her into the ditch, narrowly missing the vehicle that had been bearing down on her. My claws had dug deep into it's side, mangling the metal as I roared out my frustration. The little witchling had thrown me, gone after Bo.

Protect child

Dark whispers of my instinct wrapped around me tightly as I stalked into the ditch, feeling my muscles engorge and grow with my need to shift. No one was going to hurt Bo, not even the alluring red head who smelled faintly of desire. My keen eyes tried to search them out and I let loose a growl as I watched the witch crawl across the ground quickly. I bared my teeth and snapped them together, ready to pounce when she wrapped her arms around Bo and rubbed her cheek across her wet hair as if in peaceful bliss.

Rapidly crooned words escaped her mouth as she stroked the pup's arms, feeling her little fingers as she patted her head. My instinct slowly retreated and I was left wary but no longer filled with aggression towards the little witchling that seemed to be... *mothering* the pup intently. I crouched down, moving closer slowly as she patted and preened Bo, lightly scolding her for being wet and cold. Bo looked at me but she sunk close to the witch as if comforted by her presence.

"Bapa?" Her small voice yanked on my instinct and I bared my teeth, moving closer before reaching out, snagging her from the witch's arms. She gave a small cry, her arms reaching for Bo as I pulled her away. Her green eyes glimmered in the dark as runes flashed across her skin in rapid, pale pulses.

Female is distressed
Wants to hold child
Has strong instinct to mother

My instinct whispered at me and I narrowed my eyes at the witchling as Bo clung to me but reached out for the witch. The witch *was* distressed, her green eyes pleading as I held her at arm's length away from the pup. Her chin quivered as she made a low and pitiful sound, attempting to reach Bo's out stretched hand.

Female means no harm
Child safe
Allow contact

I slowly pulled my arm back, letting her close. She shuffled closer, nearly crawling as she tucked herself close to me, grasping at Bo as she pulled her to her chest. My instinct hummed at me in satisfaction and I basked in the feeling of the female near me as tending to the pup. Her magick flashed across her skin in faint pink pulses. It was strange. I had never seen a creature of the Territory wear their magick like that. A rustling sound from further away had me bristling.

Protect

I slowly eased an arm around her, looking into the dark searching for any threats. "Come." They need to be where it is safe. I attempted to pull the female but she resisted, her entire focus on Bo as she chattered to her. I tugged on her again and she once again resisted. I gave a low growl and pulled Bo away from her, leaving her in the ditch as I took the little female up to the road. It was not safe where we were.

A pitiful sound escaped the female and I tuned it out, even when Bo wiggled in my arms echoing it. "I have a cabin you two can stay at for a bit. If you wanted." Her voice was a tiny little waver, the sound of nearly lost in the rain. I stopped and slowly turned around, her arms were wrapped around her middle as she stared at me, her green eyes wide with longing. The female seemed... lonely.

It was odd. Witches lived in compounds, always surrounded by others. There was no reason for this one to feel lonely...unless the rumours about warlocks were true. They weren't being born much like werefemales. I narrowed my eyes, she could be luring me into a trap, bringing me to her cabin and letting me get ambushed by the enemies that sought us out. I bared my teeth as her, a feral growl rumbling my chest.

"Lying, witchling." I turned around and started off into the darkness. I needed to cover more ground, they would catch up to us otherwise. Bo's protection came first before all.

"*Wait!* Don't leave!" Her voice had taken a slight pitch of panic. "You are the first person I've had an actual conversation with in months. A-and she's the first child I have seen in even longer." Her voice sounded pained on that last sentence as if it had been a cruel punishment for her. My instinct hissed and growled at the thought, denying a mothering female a child was wrong, no matter the species.

"If you are worried about witches being around, don't. I was banished." She sounded a bit bitter as she said the word but it was enough to make me stop. "No one comes out this far. It's just me at the cabin." A witchling female alone out in the edges of the Territory.

It seemed laughable. Warlocks and the Elder witches kept them tucked away in the compounds, far away from any werewolves. She was a young witchling, perhaps in her twenties and she was fair, unbelievably so. Easy pickings for any male that would come her way. My instinct curled around my spine.

Protect female
Perhaps she will give reward

A female alone out in the wilderness without a male to guide her away from danger. I wondered what reward she would give me. If I hadn't been mistaken I had scented interest on her when she had caught sight of me. I felt my lips curl upwards at that. I had not had a female in a long time and she was far more comely than the last. I slowly turned around and her gaze immediately landed on Bo, an intense longing flooded those green, almost glowing, eyes of hers.

"Alone?" The word was low and rasping and she nodded, coming closer as if drawn towards me. I could bend this female to my will if she was that intent on mothering Bo. She would do much for the child if my instinct was guiding me true and it had never been wrong before.

"No one else." She shifted on her feet, her mesmerizing eyes flicking to my face and away from Bo, but I could see her twitching with the effort as if fighting her instinct. "Can you fix vehicles?" Her eyes darted to the rusty truck that she had been driving.

My instinct snarled at the look of it. It was not a safe mode of transportation. The female was not well off alone. She was lucky we had stumbled on her.

I shrugged, letting my eyes trail over her form, I hadn't been wrong in my first or second look. She had a body made for breeding. Small waist, flaring hips, and a set of breasts that looked to be begging for hands to hold them. I shifted on my feet, trying to ease the sudden ache in my groin as her form made my shaft harden.

I gave a small grunt, "Passable at it." I doubted there was much I could do to help the death trap she had been driving.

"Okay. My truck needs some work, as payment for you staying?" She tucked her red hair behind ear and I watched as her eyes lit up with... excitement? The little witching must have been truly lonely if she was excited about the prospect of being in the presence of a werewolf.

Our species had no love between them. All the witches I had come across were either aggressive or coldly civil. They held masks to their faces to hide their intentions.

I bared my teeth at the thought of her expressions being merely a mask. "*Fine.*" I gritted the word out and from how her full lips tugged into an immediate smile I doubted she was capable of a mask.

She moved towards me quickly, the runes pulsating with that pink colour.

Witchling is pleased

I felt my lip turn up at the corner as I let her take Bo from my arms. Her emotions were painted on her skin, they pulsated with colours. This little witchling could not deceive me. My instinct and I rumbled our satisfaction at the knowledge. I reached out, grasping her waist and tucking her close. She seemed to ignore me as she cooed at Bo happily, a faint yellow mixing with the pink as both pulsed from the magick embedded in her skin.

She didn't resist me as I lead her towards the rusty truck. I narrowed my eyes at it once more as my instinct hissed. Vehicles were no good in my opinion and I knew the one I was looking at was barely passable at the best of times. My instinct was hesitant with it and so was I but the little witchling didn't seem to hesitate as she pulled open the passenger door. The screaming of the hinges made me want to cover my ears. It was too piercing and I snapped my teeth in agitation.

"You can drive right?" Green eyes looked up at me from her position on the seat and I narrowed my eyes as I trailed them down to where she cradled Bo to her chest. She looked natural with a pup pressed to her chest and my instinct slithered in a new direction with her.

Breed female

I fought the instinct on that thought. There was a time for it and as much as I wanted to bury myself in her curvy form and lose myself in what I knew would be a receptive body I had to get where it was safe.

Protect first

Breed later

"Were?" She looked up at me, her head tilting and I shook my head to clear the thoughts away. I reached forward and grabbed the seat belt, leaning over her to click it in place. I could feel her breathing quicken as I forced myself into her space, that faint scent of interest came once again and my eyes went hooded.

She was *receptive*.

I pulled away from her and watched as her tongue peeked out to touch her bottom lip. I fought back a groan at the sight of it and the images it inspired.

"I take that as a yes?" Her voice was breathy and her eyes were slowly lowering as they landed on my mouth. I felt my mouth quirk up at the side before I gave a sharp nod as I pulled out of the cab completely and closed the door.

I lifted my head towards the rain and inhaled deeply, scenting for those who followed me in search of the pup. My lip curled at the thought of it. Bo was under my protection, no harm would come to her as long as I lived. I moved around the truck, my eyes darting back and forth, searching the darkness for anything to watch out for. There was nothing out there, not yet but I knew one of the times I looked there would be.

Kill them all

Dark thoughts from my dark instinct. I bared my teeth in pleasure of doing just that. My enemies would not find their prey, they would find a predator that would protect what was his.

16

Chapter Three
Poor Banishment

I stroked the child's damp hair and happiness wrapped around me as the need inside of me was satisfied. Children were an intense need for me. I needed to just touch them and it was fulfilled. It was an intense need that burned my very skin the longer I went without touching a child that was near. This one sat on my lap, content with my petting and patting.

Such a sweet little thing.

I glanced at the werewolf that was driving the truck and bit my lip slightly. Fuck he was fine. His hair was longer than I was used to but all I could think about was running my hands through it as he feasted on me. I clenched my legs together tightly as I watched as his muscles bulged as he inhaled deeply.

Such sensitive noses they had. My mouth wanted o quirk up but I pushed the urge down and away as I turned back to the little girl. "What is your name, sweetheart?" I chucked her chin and her nearly glowing eyes looked up at me with such a stark innocence that it made me want to pepper her face with kisses and wrap her up in bubble wrap to keep her safe from the world.

"Bo." It was a faint whisper and I smiled at her.

"Bo is a very nice name. My name is Miranda but everyone calls me BamBam." Everyone being myself.

I didn't have a lot of friends.

One didn't make friends with witches when one was content to fuck with all the rules. It didn't bother me much, they were all stuck up assholes anyway, not worth the time and effort. Especially with how most of them liked to fuck with my younger sister, Lacey. I shook the thoughts away and watched as the little werefemale mouthed my name. I nodded happily before giving her a tight hug.

I loved children. I really did. Holding her made me feel content and happier than I had in years. Children were rare in the Covens the single witches were forced to live in. She was the first one I had touched in years.

"Ren." The growling rumble that made my body shiver came from the large male sitting behind the steering wheel.

"Ren." I rolled his name around in my mouth as if tasting it. I wanted to shudder because that name felt sinful on my tongue. Witches and weres weren't allowed to mix. It was one of the big four. The four big rules of our kind that could get you jailed, banished, or killed.

Never use emotions or unpurified tools to cast magick.

Never go leave the compounds or go to the Territories without an escort.

Never take off your contraceptive spell outside of specified reasonings.

*And **never** fuck a werewolf.*

19

The way things were going I was going to break one of them. I was banished so I was technically not a part of the law system anymore but if someone found out I was lusting after a beautiful hunk of weremale called Ren, I would be burned at the stake.

The oldest trick in the book.

Burn the witch.

It was what they did to Rowenya Stoneheart. She had gotten preggers by a werewolf by the name of Ragnor. He dumped her, the kid died before it was three months old, and right before they burned her alive for the crime of loving a werewolf. She cast herself a nasty little curse on the werewolves that somehow managed to bounce back on her own species. No one ever said using emotions to fuel one's magick as going to result in a perfectly predictable spell. She was probably the reason the first rule existed in the first place and was therefor the reason I was banished.

I didn't care. The witch had mad respect from me. She managed to fuck over two species and spit in the face of those lighting her pyre. A bad bitch like that deserved all the respect in the world. She was my personal hero. I mean what rebel *wouldn't* idolize a female who had broken so many rules they created new ones just because of her? A rather shitty one in my personal opinion.

They used to teach her to us as a cautionary tale about the evils of the weres but I was always more impressed by her than the fact we were cursed by her. The tales did their best to spin the weres as evil creatures who were responsible for our woes but I knew it was stupidity that caused that. They took a grieving witch, denied her a chance at vengeance to kill the werewolf who duped her, and then burned her at the stake. I am positive if they had let her merc the asshole on her own terms then there wouldn't have been a curse to begin with.

Everyone who believed in that tail was stupid in my opinion. It was only logical to come to that conclusion but they were intent on blaming werewolves like they had since burning Rowenya six hundred years before. I guessed they were a little pissed about the whole curse backfiring and Warlocks not being born thing going on. I mean witches were fucking fertile. I could look at a picture of sperm and get pregnant.

That is if my contraceptive spell wasn't on. Handy little thing let me get laid safely so many times. No unwanted pregnancies for me and no males to follow me around because of a baby bump.

Although those feelings were disappearing the longer I held Bo. I did want kids. I wanted little crawling magick filled babies. When I was focused on sex then it was fine to push the need for children but when one was confronted with a little one, it was impossible to push away. As if to punctuate the thought, Bo snuggled closer to me, melting me into a little pile of goo. She was just too cute.

I stroked her hair, letting her snuggle in closer. She smelled like dirt and rain and I knew she would be needing a bath when we got back to my cabin. As shitty as it was, my magick made it livable. A few illegal portal doors and some inter-dimensional magick made it a... roomier experience. To be honest my cabin was better than the coven I had lived in. At least there I didn't have people checking my room for contraband items or warlocks. Life in a coven was horridly tedious but at least there I had some human interaction.

Although by the looks of things, I was going to get a lot more than human interaction because the way Ren was looking at me was not in a way that made me think he wanted to simply talk. In fact he looked like he had a far better use of his mouth in mind. I squeezed my thighs together at the thoughts it inspired, ignoring the sound the weremale let out as he inhaled.

It wasn't any fun if I couldn't tease him. I was a favourite for some males, magickal or other wise, and it didn't have anything to do with my personality. I could drive a male crazy without even touching him. It was a skill I had perfected, that is also why I got so agitated when they didn't reciprocate.

Which is also why I was still so pissed off about my banishment. My banishment had been because of some shitty warlock who was shitty in bed.

Who got banished for *that?*

I didn't even create chaos or ruin a coven permanently. I blew up a witch because her warlock was a sack of shit. It was lack lustre and I was disappointed in myself. I *knew* I was better than that but I wasn't allowed to have a do over. I had to deal. It sucked but that was the way shit ended up. I also wasn't about to go back in time, that made shit all sorts of wonky. I shuddered at the thought, I tried that once and *never again.*

A small hand tapped my cheek lightly and I looked down at Bo, a soft smile crossing my face as I lifted my legs up slightly, curling around her. I loved kids and I wondered if it was in my blood, my mother was very affectionate to all the children she had. She seemed happiest pregnant and surrounded by her children.

Ten daughters and only one son.

I still remembered when she had my little brother, my father had *finally* paid attention to her. He was a douche to the highest order. I never saw the warlock growing up. I always suspected he had a harem somewhere but my mother insisted just said he was busy.

"I'm hungry." Bo's voice was tiny and I made a faint sound in my throat. I could hear her stomach growling and I immediately thought about what I had in the fridge that I could make into a decent meal for the little sweetheart. I knew I had at least enough to make a grilled cheese sandwich.

"When we get to my cabin I'll make you a grilled cheese. Does that sound yummy?" I smiled at her but she just blinked at me blankly as if she didn't understand what I had said. I frowned slightly. "Grilled cheese, like the sandwich you fry? You *have* had one before right?" She shook her head and my heart ached for the sweet little thing. "Don't you worry, when we get there I'll make you one." She smiled up at me and pressed her face into my chest, nuzzling me with a happy sigh.

The poor little female must not have had a lot of things out in the wilderness with Ren. That was no life for a baby, they needed to be spoiled and well taken care of. I knew my babies would have rounded chubby cheeks that spoke of just how much I took care of them and spoiled them rotten. She was looking a little too thin and I made a mental note to fix that. While she was in my reach she would have perfectly rounded cheeks that begged to be pinched.

23

A large hand gripped my thigh tightly and I inhaled sharply, my eyes immediately landing on Ren. He was staring out the front window and I was faintly aware of the tap of his claws against my thigh as he held it in his grip. "Where do I go?" His voice was low and I tried my hardest to ignore just how much I loved having his hand on me as I looked out the windshield.

It was hard to think because all I could imagine was his hand on my bare thighs as he shoved me down onto my bed, his eyes looking up at me as he got ready to *devour* me.

The prick of his claws grew a bit sharper and a low rumble escaped him. "*Witchling.*" There was a warning to his tone that made my skin tighten and my breasts feel achy and heavy.

"Two miles up you turn left." My voice was nearly breathless and I looked over at him as he removed his hand from my thigh, leaving the spot almost throbbing with awareness. I knew my cheeks and chest were flushed with my interest for him and I knew that he could smell it on me.

Honestly all I wanted him to smell on me was himself when I got through with him. I just knew from looking at him that he was a male that made sure his females were... *well* satisfied and after the dry spell I had. I needed that.

Chapter Four
Happy Home

We pulled up to the front of my cabin and Ren was silent as he stared at it. I felt a bit put out at his silence. I knew it was rundown looking on the outside, some might have even called it dilapidated, but one couldn't judge it until they saw the inside of it. My cabin definitely didn't look as rundown on the inside as the outside suggested.

"Live *here?*" There was an edge to Ren's deep and rumbling voice that had me shivering as I adjusted my arm around Bo so I could open the truck door.

"Better than sleeping out in the woods like an animal." I said the insult rather lazily as I looked towards him. His eyes flashed at me with that sheen of feral intention as his teeth bared at me. "Don't judge it, it's quaint." I pushed open the door, not missing how he twisted his head as the piercing sound of the rusted hinges screamed into the night air.

I held the little girl in my arms as I stepped out of the truck. The night air smelled damp, earthy, and heavenly. I knew there was a witching moon out, I could feel its magick tingling against my skin. It was a perfect night and normally I would be out casting a myriad of spells to keep my levels normal but I had more pressing things to attend to. Namely the little female named Bo who was hungry and filthy.

I jostled her in my arms slightly. "Let's get you cleaned up and fed." She made no sound as she wrapped her arms around my neck and laid her head on my shoulders. I wanted to squeeze her tight and never let her go, she was just so cute.

I carried her towards the cabin, ignoring the weremale as I did so. He could do as he wished. I had a baby to take care of first and foremost.

"You are just going to *love* grilled cheese." I was excited to show her something she had never had before. I frowned slightly though, her damp clothes were soaking into me and I could feel her shivering. "You are going to love having a warm bath as well." There was no way I was going to let her be cold when I could run her a wonderful and warm bath. I was going to straight up pamper her.

I felt really giddy at that thought as I shifted her in my arms so I could push open my cabin's front door. The interior immediately brightened and Bo lifted her head off my shoulder, looking around with wide eyes.

"Not too bad, huh, baby?" I knew I had made the space livable. It was a mixture of modern and country couture. I mean I didn't exactly pay for any of it. I had magick fingers that happened to be very sticky at times.

I smirked slightly as I carried Bo to the bathroom. I never claimed to be a *good* witch, just a very powerful one. I waved my hand at the stove, runes flaring down my arm to my hand as the pans in the kitchen rattled, listening to my silent command.

Bo stared at the open kitchen with amazement, her eyes shining with her animalistic curiosity as my magick took control of the kitchen to make her, her food.

I pushed open a heavy black door and a light flashed on as a white bathroom appeared in the previously dark space as the inter-dimensional door's magic kicked in.

"Looky here, Bo!" I set her down on the edge of the tub before I reached over and turned on the taps. Warm water immediately came out and steam slowly curled into the air as I pushed the plug down. "Let's get you out of those wet clothes and into a warm bath." I helped pull her damp sweater off and tossed it to the side before I helped her out of the rest of her clothes.

I lifted her up and settled her into the bath as I grinned, kneeling next to the tub as I rested my arms on the side of it. "Do you want some bubbles?" Bo giggled as she swished the water with her hand and nodded. I reached down and trailed my fingers through the warm water. My magick bubbled out of me as my runes flashed a happy blue.

Bubbles immediately started forming in the water and Bo gave a happy giggle as she played with them. "Nice and warm, right?" She was still shivering but seemed to be very content in the water. I smiled as I watched her. There was something deep inside of me that settled taking care of her.

I *ached* for children. I might have been a rebel but like Rowena I loved kids. She had died trying to get vengeance for her child's death, for the weremale abandoning them both. We were kind of notoriously monogamous when we set our minds to it. Which made it difficult for me in my want for children.

I could be with a human if I really wanted too, or a fey if I was into the weirdness of how inhuman they looked at times, but tradition and rules dictated I needed to be with a warlock and those were getting to be mighty short in supply and they never cared about their partners. I had seen enough and fucked enough to know that. Warlocks were fucking assholes who knew they didn't have to do much of anything to have the choice witches they wanted.

I was always lucky because being a level seven witch I was considered a boon to any warlock who wanted me. I was powerful and would have made an Elder in my own right as I ruled over a coven.

I let out a faint sigh as Bo picked up a handful of bubbles. I hated rules and Elders lived strictly by the rules. I didn't want anything to do with that, I never did, it was what made me so difficult to deal with. The way our world was, irritated me. There was no freedom to be who we wanted. We were assigned roles and places and we were expected to never deviate. I deviated and I got punished, as stupid as the reason for it was, I still got punished.

I could feel my magick in the kitchen coming to an end and I stood up before waving my hand, a small bucket materialized and I handed it to Bo. "Get your hair wet, baby. I'll wash it when I get back." I got up and moved to the doorway right as Ren walked in from outside. I immediately bit my lip as I stared at him. The rain had caused his shirt to stick to his form and mama was liking what she was seeing. He looked carved from granite and every edge was lovingly crafted. Seeing him in the dark paled very much in comparison to seeing him in actual lighting.

He lifted his head and inhaled deeply before he moved towards the stove. "Ah ahhhh." I immediately moved into the main space and squeezed myself between him and the grilled cheese I had made for Bo. I was nearly pressed up against his chest as he let out a faint rumble. I walked my hand up his chest with a sly smile as my blood heated in my veins. "You don't get to eat this one. It's for Bo." As delicious as he was, babies came first.

The runes pulsated a faint red with my heavy interest in him as he pressed his hands to the edge of the stove beside me, caging me in. He dropped his head, inhaling deeply before he gave a rumbling growl that made goosebumps erupt over my skin.

"But if a weremale wants a meal..." I slowly looked up at him as my hand reached his collar bone. "All he has to do is ask." I couldn't help how throaty my voice turned, how I arched towards him as if completely on instinct. I liked this male and I would be hard pressed not to take him for a ride around the world. This male wouldn't leave my bed for *days*.

He captured my wrist in one of his large hands and my eyes went half-lidded in pleasure at his touch. "*Witchling.*" The word was nearly garbled from all the rumbling growls that excited his chest before he pressed his face into my neck and inhaled deeply. I whimpered and arched my back just a touch further until my chest touched his and a heavy flushed coated my cheeks and chest as I let out a faint groan.

It had been far too long since I had a male pressed up against me like that and it wasn't fair. "Kill us if they find out." He scrapped his canines across the delicate skin of my throat and I inhaled sharply. The edge of danger that flared up with the action only enhanced my desire. He could tear out my throat and there would be nothing I could do about it and *fuck* did that turn me on.

I reached out with my other hand, grasping the waistband of his jeans before tugging him closer. "I won't tell if you won't." I purred out the words, tasting them on my tongue. I didn't care about the consequences to my actions. I never did. It was what made me, me and if he thought I was going to bitch out because some Elder witches would try and burn me at the stake for learning every inch of his body then he was in for a fun lesson because I never bitched out.

Ever.

He gave a deep and percussive growl that vibrated my chest and sent a flood of heat through me. I imagined him doing that while between my legs and I gave a faint moan. Who needed batteries with him around? However the sloshing of water in the tub reminded me of what I was doing and I gently pushed him away. He gave an aggravated sound deep in his throat as I turned around. I flicked my wrist at the cupboard and a plate was immediately in my hands before I slid the grilled cheese onto it.

Hot hands grasped my hips and Ren tugged me against him, pressing his arousal into my ass with a harsh growl as if to say I created it so I would have to deal with it. Despite how my entire body clenched and vibrated at the thought I merely turned my head and kissed him on his shadowed jaw with a grin.

"Babies before boys." I patted his cheek softly. "Go take a look at the truck." I darted underneath his arm and headed straight for the bathroom, making sure to swish my hips in a way that I knew would grab his attention and from the choked off growl he gave, the weremale was standing at *full* attention.

Chapter Five
Teaser

I growled as I shoved open the hood of the truck. The female was vexing. My cock ached so hard I felt like I had been kicked. She was enticing and alluring and *interested*. Rain started to patter down around me once more and I gave another heavy rumble.

Feast
Give female what she wants

I rolled my head slightly, tensing as my instinct stirred the beast inside of me. It never came out unless called and the female named BamBam was playing with fire and she would end up burned. What was worse was she seemed to *know* that and did so anyway, heedless of the danger it represented.

Vexing female. I bared my teeth as I looked over the dirty motor. I could see some of the belts were fraying they were so worn and my instinct hissed at them.

Female is in danger
Destroy truck

It was so simple for my instinct. It always pointed me to the most direct route but I knew there was more than that. The female was stubborn, stubborn enough that she could negate her own interest for me to tend to Bo. She was practically shaking for me to sate her and yet she had pushed me away. I knew a female like that would not forgive a transgression such as destroying her only means of transport. Not only that she was so far away from anything I didn't wish to leave her stranded.

Bo and I would move on, we always did. It was easier to keep moving to keep Bo safe but even my instinct was hesitant in leaving the female without means of escape. She was a witch, a powerful one that could work magic straight from her hands, but we would not leave her without transport, no matter how shitty that transport was.

I grimaced as I checked the fluid levels, reaching down to adjust my aching cock, trying to find a comfortable spot for the engorged appendage. I wanted to redden her ass for her teasing but the thought of my hand on her round ass made my cock stiffen further and I let out a heavy groan. I tilted my head up to the rain and closed my eyes. I hated the rain. It cloaked scents and left me unable to scent where our enemies were but I was hoping it was cold enough to lessen my hard on.

"Do you need anything, Ren?" Her sultry voice shoved my mind back into where I had her pressed up against me, her satin voice telling me if I wanted something to eat to ask her. My cock throbbed painfully and I looked at her over my shoulder, my eyes narrowing as I looked at her. She crossed her arms over her chest, her plump lips pulling up into a smirk. "Keep looking at me like that and I'll have to let you bend me over the nearest surface." She reached up, slipping a tip of her finger between her lips as she lightly bit it, her eyes going hooded as she looked at me

I growled heavily as I watched the action intently. "*Don't tease.*" I barred my teeth at her as I snapped them together in warning. I had never encountered such a vexing female. She was not behaving as females usually did. There was no shyness to her like the demure werefemales and no cold and hostile edge of a witch. She was all silk and heat that was begging to be wrapped around me tightly.

She slowly pulled her fingertip from between her teeth. "It's only teasing if I don't follow through." She smirked at me once more before raking her gaze over me. "I'm a *very* naughty witch, Ren... and I'm... down to break a few rules if you are." She winked at me, running a graceful and pale hand through those fiery red locks as she turned around and sashayed into the small cabin.

"Your dinner is on the table." She casually threw the words over her shoulders and I ground my teeth together, my hands clutching at the body of the truck, the metal groaning underneath my fingers.

I snapped my teeth together in agitation. That female knew nothing about what she was tempting. Weremales claimed and dominated, we took what we wanted. She might have joked about me bending over the nearest surface but for weremales, it was an *invitation*.

Feast

My instinct slithered up my spine, twisting in my bones. It urged me, hissed at me, to follow her into the cabin and pin her down until she was panting for me before I slid deep inside her. I rolled my head on my shoulders as I let out a heavy growl, trying to stare intently at the motor. She was a *vexing* female. I let the truck go and shoved a hand through my hair, staring out into the darkness.

Enemies were all around us, both sides hunted Bo and I down. We were never safe and we always kept moving. This female was just one of many stops we would make. Even then being anywhere near her was dangerous. She was a witch, a banished one, but a witch none the less. I narrowed my eyes as I looked around once more. I still wasn't sure that it wasn't a trap. We were far from the covens buts we were still too close for me or my instinct.

Bo's safety was everything and no matter how hard my cock was and how bad it ached, if she was in danger or being found, I would risk the witch to make sure the small female was okay. She might not have been mine but she was under my protection as she had been since her birth. I bared my teeth, my canines elongating as my jaw ached. I needed to make sure the witch knew exactly where she was placed in importance. I would kill her if she was tricking me.

I slammed the truck hood closed before I stalked towards the cabin. The interior was still lit up and I shoved the door open. I expected the female to be waiting, her lips curved up into that smirk but the main room was empty. I inhaled deeply, trying to scent her but the smell of the fried bread and cheese overloaded my senses and I immediately looked around for it. My eyes zeroed in on the plate on the table that had two of the sandwiches stacked on it.

My mouth watered and I stalked towards it. Bo and I had only been eating raw meat from the animals I killed. It sustained us but I never turned down a chance at normal food. There was a white folded note on the plate and I wanted to ignore it but the faint scent of the female wafted off of it. I tilted my head as I picked it up.

There was a bright red kiss mark on the inside with the words '*I am just putting the little beauty to bed. Eat up and have yourself a shower.*'.

I tossed the note to the side and grabbed a sandwich. It was still warm and I grinned before taking a large bite out of it. The beast might not have liked the food but it would deal with it as I had to deal with eating raw meat for several months straight.

I tilted my head the other way as I flicked the note. The female hadn't been wearing lipstick before so I wondered if she had just applied it for the note. The vibrant red colour taunted me and I pictured the colour on her lips as she knelt at my feet, her hands grasping the waistband of my pants.

I bit back a heavy groan as my cock pulsed painfully against my zipper. I gave a low growl as I took another bite of the sandwich.

Vexing female!

Chapter Six
Dessert

I stroked Bo's hair, humming to her softly as she clutched the blanket to her chest. Her hair had been cut raggedly but I had managed to french braid it. She had taken my pulling and tugging on her hair rather well.

Although I believed that had a lot to do with the fact I had given her the grilled cheese and she was super intent on eating. It made me happy to feed her and make sure she was taken care of. The mothering part of me was really strong, like I didn't already fucking know that. I was half tempted to remove my contraceptive spell and jump at Ren lady bits first because of it.

I smirked at that. I would enjoy it but babies were 'consequences' to fun. I rolled my eyes at the thought. I just had to shove down my instincts because despite how I felt, and how certifiably insane I was, I didn't trust Ren entirely. And that fact alone meant no babies, no matter how much my mind and body was telling me I wanted them.

I pushed all the thoughts away as Bo's breathing evened out and she went completely limp in the bed. I smiled at her softly, stroking her cheek with the backs of my fingers. Her skin was silky and warm. I could remember my mother doing this to me as I slept in my bed.

I had been her first child and I knew she had doted on me a fair bit. I felt a small smile on my face at the thought of her. That was the one thing I missed above all else since I had been banished and that was seeing my family. I hadn't really been allowed to visit them when I had been shipped off to the coven but it was the thought that I could have visited them if I had taken the time. Now I was barred from seeing them at all. It hurt, my siblings were growing and learning, making their own way in life and I wasn't there to watch them.

I let out a small sigh, there as no reason for such sombre thoughts. I bent down and brushed her a few strands of hair from Bo's face before I kissed her cheek. "Good night, beauty. Rest well." She murmured something in a sleepy little mumble before a small smile crossed her face and she nuzzled the blanket with a sigh. I slowly crept off the bed, the lights lowering as my runes flickered a light blue.

I could hear the shower running as I slipped from the small bedroom I had conjured up for the little werefemale and my mouth twitched upwards. I closed the door gently, hearing the faint click of the lock before the light blue runes moved down my arms and to the wood of the door. They fell into precise formation, letting me know the room was secured and sound proof. We could hear Bo but Bo couldn't hear us.

Which was good because I had no intentions of being quiet. I bit my lower lip lightly. I was fucking hot and bothered because of a certain weremale. I hadn't put much thought into if I was because I hadn't had sex in a while or if he was just that divine to look at. I didn't even care. He was hot, cut, domineering, and interested. That was more than enough to get my engines purring.

I glanced at the bathroom door before looking at my bedroom door. I lightly stroked the neckline of my tank top as I pondered if I should get fully dressed down for him or continue on with what I was currently working with. I looked down, using my finger to pull my shirt away from my chest. I was wearing a lacy black ensemble that I personally liked. I never dressed my lingerie down. A girl could never be too careful of when a male might see her without her shirt on.

I made a slight face at it though. I did have an entirely fun silky red lingerie set that I knew would drive any male wild but Ren was currently in the shower and as I was planning on joining him, I didn't want to ruin the silk.

With that thought I quickly reached down and pulled my shirt off, tossing it in the general direction of my bedroom before I unbuttoned my pants and shimmied out of them. I kicked them away and with a wave of my hand a full length mirror appeared. I looked myself over, turning this way and that to make sure I looked just as sexy now as I had this morning.

I watched as the runes flashed a pretty and delighted pink across my body. I went up on my tip toes and turned, looking over my shoulder and smirking as I caught sight of my ass in the black lace. Ren was going to be driven to distraction by that sight. I gave a happy nod, satisfied that no male, were or not, would turn me down for sex. Not that I was worried any would. I knew I was fine as hell and there was no male stupid enough to tell me no. I just liked the ego boost it gave me to make sure.

I quickly waved the mirror away and looked at the bathroom door. My heart pounded in my chest as anticipation rolled through me. Ren had given me a mighty big ache that he needed to rectify. I nearly burned as I remember how big he seemed pressed against me and I lightly licked my bottom lip. I hadn't had sex in a while and I felt like such a grand cock was the *perfect* welcome back present. I arched my back slightly, my chest flushing as I walked towards the bathroom.

I glanced over my shoulder to where the white note I had written was slightly crumpled up. I smirked, it was time to serve Ren his well deserved dessert. I knew he had gotten my note and he was more than likely very frustrated over it. I knew just how to tease and press a male to make him nearly lose his mind. I loved playing this game. It made life fun and interesting.

I didn't hesitate as I flicked my wrist, runes flaring, and the door unlocked and allowed me entrance. The air was steamy and I could feel the moisture kissing my skin softly as I looked to the shower curtain. I could see his hazy figure behind the curtain and I bit my lower lip as I slowly leaned against the door, letting it click shut.

The sound seemed to hang in the air as male showering froze, a dark and deadly sounding rumble emerging from him. It rolled over my body, sending shivers down my limbs, tightening my nipples, and creating a heated slickness in my core.

I arched my back my mouth twitching as he shoved the curtain back and launched at me. His hand landed around my throat, that sound vibrating the air between us as his eyes gleamed his feral nature. His grip tightened a fraction, restricting very little but the tightness was a firm reminder that his hand was there.

Not that I needed the reminder, his skin was rough and hot against mine. It was like a heavy brand that had me arching my back even as I lazily grinned at his feral expression.

"Kill you." The words were a growled rumble and I raised an eyebrow, trying very hard to be a good girl and look at his face rather than letting my gaze wander but from the water drops slowly making their way down his delightfully cut form it was very, *very* hard. His fingers tightened a bit more, bringing my attention back to his face. "You betray us. I will kill you." His expression was dark and his gaze held a heated promise of death and retribution with his words and I found myself smiling at the rather adorable threat.

"Like wise." This poor male had absolutely no idea who he was dealing with. He couldn't just kill me. He could threaten it but doing it was a much harder task. I slowly stuck my bottom lip out in a playful pout before I reached up, walking my fingers down the arm holding my neck. "But are you *really* going to threaten me when I was so nicely bringing you your dessert?" I blinked at him before pushing against the hand holding my throat so I could come closer to him. "You'd like it. It's *silky*...." I breathed the words close to his ear.

I brushed my lips over the bottom of his ear, liking the faint grunt he gave at the contact. "It's *warm*..." His fingers twitched on my throat and I slowly tapped my fingers across his pectoral before trailing my fingers downwards.

I relished in the feeling of his muscles bunching underneath his skin as I touched him. "It's *sweet...*" I fairly purred the word at him as I neared the warmth of his straining cock. I didn't need to see it to know it was hard and more than likely aching like I was. "All you have to do is *eat.*" I tapped my forefinger gently against the tip of his swollen crown and he gave a hard snarl, his free hand grabbing my wrist and shoving it against the door next to my head.

His gaze was nearly wild and I felt a thrill move through me at the sight of it. I was tired of restraint. I had dealt with males who held themselves back, never giving in and letting loose. I wanted to know what pure, unadulterated, unrestricted passion and lust felt like. Even if it was just once. Plus I just *really* wanted to get laid.

I was breathing heavy as I looked into his dark eyes. He was half animal, half man, a combination that I should have balked from but instead all I wanted to do was arch into him and *beg* him to touch my skin. I swallowed, my throat moving underneath his wide palm and his gaze fell to it as he slowly removed his hand.

I wanted to whimper at the loss of contact before he grabbed my other wrist, pinning it beside my head, his gaze never once leaving my throat.

There was a faint note of fear to the vulnerable position I was in, to the feral intensity that was being directed my defenceless throat, but I shuddered as it mixed in the intensity of the situation. It sparked an intense high for the pleasure that rolled through me, forcing it to be tad sharper in my veins. It was an unbearable itch underneath my skin that was starting to fray at my control.

He dipped his head and my breathing hitched in my throat as sharply pointed canines dragged across my throat, a warning of the danger they could do as they pressed against where my pulse thumped wildly underneath my skin. I rolled my hips forward, needing contact as the faint pain of the scratches made that sharp pleasure even more jagged. My breathing deepened to pants as I lifted my chin, baring the entire expanse of my throat for him as he pulsed against my belly like a hot brand.

A sudden rumble shook his chest as both his hands left my wrists and an arm was wrapped around my back, a hot hand grabbed my ass before I was tugged against him hard. The hand on my ass stroked and squeezed my flesh, making my chest flush with desire and my breasts ache. I wanted that touch lower and between my legs where I knew I was soaking for him, *burning* for him.

Teeth suddenly pinched my neck and I inhaled quickly. "Ren." It was a faint gasp I hadn't expected to let out. He pulled back quickly, dark eyes piercing into mine for a brief moment, his nostrils flaring before he crushed his lips to mine.

His kiss was forceful and claiming. He didn't wait to be asked, he didn't hastily pucker his lips and kiss just to shut me up, he didn't do it out of obligation. He was kissing me like he wanted me to feel the intensity of his passion, like he was taking what he wanted and without asking because he knew I wanted it just as much, like he had abandoned societal modesty and went straight for pure instinct and animalistic pleasure.

Finally!

I let out a heavy groan, wrapping my arms around his neck, opening up to him, lapping my tongue against his as it shot forward. His hand tightened on my ass, claws teasingly poking my flesh as he ground himself against my stomach, his chest rumbling against mine. The sensation tickled slightly and I wanted to giggle but the thought was derailed as he shifted his mouth on mine, pressing closer. His kiss almost bruising as he twined his tongue with mine. I buried my hands into his wet hair, holding onto the damp strands tightly, pressing myself closer to him.

Heat radiated from him and sunk into me like the water on his skin. My lingerie was getting damp and I found it to be too confining. My breasts ached and the damp lace rubbed against my nipples, almost hurting the sensitive tips. I quickly let his hair go as I reached behind me.

He pulled back from my mouth and I gave a small sound of irritation before I grabbed the back of his neck and pulled him down for another kiss, our breath mingling as I flicked my tongue against his. I leaned against him, almost forgetting my one armed struggle with my bra clasp. I fiddled with the clasp for a few moments before I gave a sharp groan as I failed to undo it. I reluctantly pulled away from him as I quickly used my other hand and unclasped it.

Ren let me go and before I could protest the removal of his hands on me, he reached up and pulled my bra down. He yanked it away from my body with a growl before he bent down and wrapped his arms underneath my ass and moved us backwards. My back met the door as he lifted his head, looking up at me for a brief moment. His mouth twitched upwards just a fraction before he buried his face between my breasts, huffing against my skin as I wrapped my legs around his waist as best as I could with his arms holding my thighs.

His grip on me shifted so that he was holding my ass in both of his hot palms as he pressed an open mouth kiss to the inside of my breast. My breath escaped me in sharp exhale at the action and he huffed against my skin once more before a familiar feeling of sharp points trailed against my skin. I looked down and my breath hitched in my chest. It was one thing to feel his sharp teeth against my skin but to see it was an added thrill that had me wiggling against him with need.

My heart pounded and my mouth felt dry as I watched him nip those dangerously sharp teeth over my sensitive skin. He glanced up at me, his eyes holding me captive as he drug a sharp point over my nipple and a straggled sound escaped me as pleasure shot through me hard and fast. I had no time to react to that before he lapped at the peak before drawing it into his mouth with a hungry sounding growl. My hands grabbed his head and I didn't know whether to push him away at the almost painfully intense sensation or hold him closer demanding more of it.

My runes pulsed a hard and heavy red, my magick flickering through me almost uncontrollably. I had enjoyed sex before. I had but this was... this was so far off the scale I didn't know what the fuck to call it. His teeth teased and tormented my sensitive flesh while his hot tongue soothed the painful scratches on my skin before he released my breast from his mouth.

I was nearly gasping by the time he did so and his eyes narrowed at me a fraction before he looked at my other breast with interest. I gave a low whine, wanting to tell him to not even think about it and let me recover from the intense onslaught but being unable to say a word as I hopelessly writhed against him.

He kept eye contact with me as he lapped at my other nipple and I let out a deep groan before I saw his sharp canines. He titled his head a fraction and I panted helplessly. "Don't you dare!" My words lacked conviction and he gave me a feral grin, baring those sharp points for me in their entirety before he latched onto my breast, his teeth sinking in but not puncturing my skin. I let out a yelp of slight pain and he immediately released his bite, his talented and teasing tongue replacing it, soothing the sting and sending that familiar burn through me.

I managed to catch my breath and glared down at him as he released the skin of my breast, leaving the skin reddened and flushed, and giving my throbbing peak one last teasing lick. "When I said I was bringing you dessert that didn't meant you could actually try and eat *me*, you asshole." I cuffed him playfully upside the head.

He gave a slow shrug, his muscles rippling underneath his skin. "You taste good." He looked at me as he hoisted me a bit higher, his hands and fingers flexing on my ass before tightening in a greedy grope before he licked the underside of my breast, trailing his tongue up to flick against my nipple. I exhaled quickly at the action, wiggling in his grip. He dropped me and I gasped at the feeling of falling before he caught me when I was eye level with him, his cock shoved right up against the fabric of my panties. I had to fight to keep my eyes from rolling to the back of my head at the sensation it caused.

I breathed out heavily as I glowered at him. "I should zap your balls off for that." My heart thudded in my chest and he bent down, nipping at my bottom lip as he drug ones of his hands down my thigh, gripping and stroking my skin, sending waves of intense heat over me.

"Would be a favour. They hurt." He seemed unfazed by that even as he throbbed heavily against my core.

I licked my lips, looking down to where the swollen crown was. "I could fix that." I *wanted* to fix that. I could practically taste him on my tongue and it nearly made my mouth water.

He gave a shake of his head, surprising me. "Not done with my dessert yet." His eyes raked over me as his fingers dug into my rounded ass, his gaze was clearly on the black lace panties I was wearing as his nostrils flared once more.

"You would turn down a *mind blowing* blow job because you want to continue to bite me?" I raised an eyebrow and my only response was a short shake of his head.

"Not bite..." He slowly looked up and the look in his eyes was full of wild intensity. "*Eat.*" That word said all I needed to know and I blinked at him. He turned down a blow job because the big bad werewolf wanted to eat *me* out. I felt a little stunned.

I had hit the mother fucking jackpot of males. I didn't really know how to respond and he didn't seem to care as the bathroom door opened and he carried me out of the steamy room. I had a faint forethought to wave my hand behind him, shutting everything off in the small room.

He held me close and he walked quickly, his strides overtaking the small kitchen and heading straight for my bedroom. A rumble of a chuckle escaped his chest and his brushed his lips over my jaw before he teased my skin with those canines. I pressed myself closer to him, baring my neck as I wrapped my arms around his neck. I wanted him closer than he currently was. I wanted him inside me, I wanted him under my skin so he could sooth that harsh and jagged itch that rolled through my veins.

I could fucking understand why Rowena hopped on the were dick train. He hadn't even touched my real fun parts and he had already blown all the competition out of the water. Not that they were a really high bar to begin with but now that I knew there was an even higher standard than my previous one I was fucking pissed I hadn't discovered it sooner. Instead of listening to the Elders preach about the heinousness of werewolves I should have been out playing little red to their big bad wolves in the most decidedly *not* fairy tale way.

The dim lighting of my bedroom enveloped us and the scent of herbs sunk into me, relaxing me and heating up my form at the same time. I liked keeping a certain ambience in my private domain and from how Ren was stiffening I didn't doubt he was picking up on that.

I was rather ungracefully tossed onto the bed and I dropped my mouth open in slight anger. "You can't just toss a lady around! It's not nice!" I glowered at him but he seemed to not be listening entirely as he knelt by the bed reaching out and grasping my thighs.

51

Anticipation coiled in my stomach before he yanked me closer. He shoved his shoulders between my legs, spreading me open to his gaze.

I watched him with interest as my breathing deepened. That animalistic gleam to his eyes seemed to sear into me as he rubbed his cheek against my inner thigh, nipping at the sensitive skin almost lazily. The male had an inherent fascination with dragging his teeth across my skin. Not that I was complaining... well maybe a little.

I looked at my breasts, there were red lines criss-crossing them from his attentions. I could even see a few lines from where he had pressed too hard and had actually scratched my skin.

I reached up, trailing my finger across one of the lines, there was no pain from them and I shivered, goosebumps erupting over my skin as my feather light touches. I tapped the skin of my breast, watching it bounce slightly with a bit of amusement as I shifted my legs slightly on Ren's shoulders. I pulled my gaze from my breasts to look at him only to realize he was staring at me intently, his eyes focused on the actions of my hands.

I raised an eyebrow as I continued to tap my breast. "Look at what you did to my poor girls. They look *ravished*." They felt ravished as well, deliciously so at that. I shifted my leg on his shoulder to knock my knee against the side of his head gently. "They are accustomed to a gentle touch. Like this." I softly cupped one, stroking the skin gently with my fingers and he gave a small snort.

"A male marks skin to remind you he was there." He locked his eyes with mine as he drug a canine down my inner thigh, leaving a red mark behind. Pleasure spiked through me, muting the pain and burning my desire higher. "Uses gentle hand to hide he was between your legs." He rubbed his cheek against the mark he just made, a smirk on his mouth that showcased his utter smug satisfaction with him. "I'm proud, so I mark." I bit my lip at that.

Sexy male.

He gave a heated chuckle as he looked at me. "You like my marks." He bent closer to me, so close to my sex that I could feel his breath brushing the fabric of my lacy panties. "I can *smell* it." He inhaled deeply and I grinned at him, he had absolutely no shame and that was utterly perfect in my opinion.

"You know how many males I had to threaten to get into your current position?" Far too many.

Warlocks didn't like to reciprocate oral. I was learning there was very little they liked to do to witches and it was fucking grating. I had been missing out on great sex for years.

Ren hadn't even dipped in yet and this was already surpassing every other partner I had been with… well except one. Landon the human had taken me for a rather great ride but he hadn't looked at my sex with a feral and hungry gaze. So points off of the human and points tacked on for Ren the were.

"Warlocks not men." His voice was low and growled, the vibrations shuddering the air between us. I could tell he had little respect of the males of my species as his eyes narrowed. "They greedy. They gorge on witches for their own pleasure and never think about them after." His eyes glittered at they looked at me from between my legs. "If breeders are not happy then the breeding is cut off. Weres keep their breeders *very* happy." My core clenched at the possessive and dark tone he took on and I reached out and fisted the comforter in my hands as I bit my lip hard.

"Keep chatting and I might think weres are all talk and no game." I was tired of the chit chat, his breath against my core was driving me crazy and I wanted to be sated immediately. I had very little patience for the sharp ache that was growing almost painful and I knew when I reached the point I was getting closer to, my magick lost all patience and that was never pretty. Already it was starting to flutter slightly amber runes down my body and towards him.

He nipped at one, my magick crackling against his teeth before fluttering back to red underneath his tongue. "Pretty." His voice was husky as he watched the now red runes dance for him on my thighs. I nudged him with my leg and raised my eyebrow when he looked at me.

Without warning he slashed my panties to ribbons and I made a disgruntled noise, ready to kick him for the wanton destruction of the expensive lingerie when his tongue probed at my slick flesh unexpectedly.

My head dropped back and I squeezed my thighs around his head as I gave a keening cry. The pleasure that had been building only twisted further as he lapped and suckled on my folds with abandon. His arms wrapped around my thighs, holding them tightly, claws scratching at my flesh as I bowed my back. My breathing was erratic and I flexed my hands before they immediately reached down, tangling my fingers in his hair as I pulled him closer to my core, demanding more.

With each lick and suckle the tension of the pleasure within me, that pounded against my skull, grew thicker and hotter. He seemed entirely intent upon his feast, completely focused on his *dessert*.

He rumbled out a sound of satisfaction and enjoyment as he flicked his tongue over my clit and had me instantly writhing in his grasp. I gasped the air I needed, my chest heaving as I managed to look down at him. His eyes met mine and there was that feral gleam that shined through the darkness of his gaze. He held me captive with his eyes, letting me see how much he enjoyed his task, how much he enjoyed the taste of me on his tongue.

I let my head drop back as I flexed my fingers in his hair, rolling my hips towards his mouth, wanting more. My belly quivered and my skin felt tight on my bones. I inhaled sharply as his tongue found my clitoris once more but instead of a teasing lick he enclosed his hot mouth over it and sucked hard. I shattered, coming hard as I pulled on his hair, rolling my hips frantically as I rode the high he had shoved me onto.

A heavy growl from him vibrated my sex and had my eyes nearly rolling back into my head from the sensation. My world grew dim from the intensity of the orgasm and I was barely aware of my surroundings as I helplessly writhed. I became faintly aware of my hands being forced above my head and a hot and heavy body resting itself between my thighs. I wrapped my legs around his waist without thinking, wanting his large body there.

My eyes snapped open and I gave a straggled scream as he slid in deep, hilting within me with one smooth stroke of his hips. Another orgasm ripped through me, my core clutching at him frantically and I twisted in his grip. The peak so intense I wasn't sure if I should beg for mercy or cry out for more.

I wasn't given a chance to choose as he pulled out and thrust back in. My mouth dropped open and he claimed my lips with his, his tongue seeking out mine intently, almost demanding in its movements.

I kissed him back eagerly, moaning into his mouth as he kept me on that high plateau of pleasure, driving me further and further with every sharp move of his hips. I wanted to touch him, to clutch at his shoulders, score his skin with my nails but I couldn't tug my wrists from his hand. He had them pinned and didn't seem inclined to let them go.

I whimpered against him, lapping at his tongue frantically as I rolled my hips up to match his thrusts. He seemed tireless as he thrust into me without mercy. I felt a sharper spike grow within me and I both dreaded and craved to be shoved into it. Craved because I was a woman of the flesh and I loved pleasure and dreaded because I was terrified this male would unmake me with the peak he was forcing me towards.

He released my mouth, pressing his lips to my throat, feeling the vibrations of my moans and cries that could now clearly be heard, no longer being muffled. I twisted my hips, sweat slickening my skin as heat flooded me in oppressive waves. Ren lowered his head, licking between my breasts with a masculine groan. I tugged against his grip on my wrists, hoping he would relent and let me go.

The heat inside of me grew to the point where it almost hurt. Everything was hot and slick and intense and I felt tears burn my eyes as my heart thudded in my chest for a few beats. Time seemed to slow down as Ren lifted his head, looking at me. His eyes were piercing and that slick pleasure he was giving me with every movement of his hips reached its tipping point.

My mouth dropped open as the pleasure shattered, rolling over me with a feral intensity that matched the one in Ren. I felt a scream building in my throat as the orgasm ripped through me. Ren captured my mouth with his, muffing the piercing sound just as it started to escape.

I tightened my legs around his waist as my sex pulsate and milked the cock he was thrusting within me. It was demanding its due from the male who's chest was starting its heavy rumble as his thrusts became more erratic and harsh.

I twined my tongue around his, nearly whimpering at the intensity of the pleasure that was rolling through me. I closed my eyes tightly, my breathing ragged and harsh before Ren groaned deep into my mouth and I could feel him coming as he thrust roughly into me, jolting my body underneath him as his cock pulsed, giving my sex what it had been begging for. My legs dropped from around his waist and spread them wide rolling my hips as as I relished in the well fucked feeling I was experiencing.

Ren nipped at my lips before rubbing his cheek against mine, his teeth nipping at the skin of my jaw as he continued to slowly rock within me. He let my wrists go and I knew I would have red marks from my struggling but I didn't care as my eyelids lowered with my satisfied exhaustion. Ren continued to draw his teeth across my skin and I shuddered, after effects still shaking me slightly even as I floated down from the peak I had been given.

Now I knew why Rowenya chose Ragnor and not a warlock because *holy shit*. That was fucking incredible. Human Landon was been boot fucked off his top spot and Ren was now smugly sitting on it with a sexy smirk and a velvet rumble in his chest.

I lifted my head, pressing a soft kiss to his shoulder, darting my tongue out to taste him. I shivered as the taste of him spread across my tongue, he tasted like sweat and primal male.

I sleepily grinned as he lifted his head, looking down at me. "Keep fucking me like that, Ren, and I might just have to keep you." He didn't respond but I didn't need him to. He could ignore me all he wanted but I was a very naughty witch and I knew ways to make a male beg me to stay.

Chapter Seven
Beast Within

The night was dark and the room was scented heavily with herbs that made my muscles relax. My instinct was still and quiet, satisfied by the fiery haired female who lay bathed in moonlight. I watched her as those runes pulsed faintly on her skin, their colour was white but so faint if I had not been watching I would not have seen them at all.

Such a strange creature she was. She liked mouthing me off even as she enjoyed what I did to her. She was also physical, liked hitting me. It was why I had her pinned down. I knew it would bother her greatly to not be able to retaliate for my marks on her skin.

I gave a low rumble of amusement at that, her pouty lips quivered as she had struggled against my hold, her eyes begging me to let her go but she was too demanding and demanding females didn't get what they wanted.

However it didn't seem to matter to her because she enjoyed the breeding just as much as I had, even demanding another one as she murmured half asleep. I was satisfied that I had made my mark on her. She would crave me again. That suited me just fine because I knew I would crave to be buried deep within her every chance that presented itself. Until such a time that we left she would be a willing bed partner and it would provide me with enough memories to keep me company on the cold nights out in the wild.

I tilted my head as I looked at her pale skin. She was a fine female, soft and delicate in her form. Looking at her asleep could make one think that she couldn't take hard hands or teeth but I knew just how well she took them, *craved* them. The remembrance of her scent in my nose and the taste of her on my tongue had my body clenching all over again.

I brushed it away as I looked around the dark room. It was the space of a pampered female. She had no male hanging around but it was clear she pampered herself regardless. Such a fine female wouldn't last out in the wilds, it was clear she loved fine silks and laces. I knew I could not fault her for that. Our own breeders were highly pampered. They were placed in lush and rich spaces, showered with anything their hearts desired if it meant allowing a single male to claim them as their breeder.

I was well aware we spoiled the females to distraction but we were simple creatures and if bestowing a female with a grand golden necklace meant we got the chance to have a breeder to continue our line, we would do so. It was why warlocks made me curl my lip up. They had so many breeders and yet they treated them poorly, banished them for breaking rules.

I was aware that I was not compatible with the female, aptly named BamBam, to produce offspring. I could smell it, the faint bitter scent that my seed would not take within her. However it did not stop me or my instinct from curling up our lips at the fact she had been banished to the outer edges of the Territory.

We knew this was no place for a breeding female, witch or otherwise. There were the worst of the species that lingered in the Outer Edges. She might have used her magic differently, been able to protect herself quicker than most but if a delinquent Fae caught her or a brutal human, there was little she could do to protect herself.

Protect her

My instinct slithered up my spine lazily and I narrowed my eyes at that. I wished to protect her as did my instinct but my duty to Bo overrode everything else. We would sacrifice the female for Bo's safety if it came to that. With that thought I stood up quickly from the bed, grabbing my jeans from the floor and shoving my legs into them. I crept from the room, moving silently through the house before I stood in front of the little female's room.

I sniffed the air experimentally as I watched the blue runes pulse on the door softly. I wasn't sure about the magick but my instinct wasn't warning me to be wary of it. My instinct never drove me wrong so I hesitantly reached out and brushed my knuckles against the door. The magick didn't strike out against me or move from its position so I relaxed, pushing the door open into the bedroom.

I looked around, scanning the room carefully. It didn't have much but I knew Bo must have appreciated the bed. She had spent most of the past few months sleeping on my back or curled up next to me. Now she curled up in a soft bed wrapped in a warm comforter. It hurt me that I couldn't give her the spoils she deserved as we escaped those who chased us.

I walked over and chucked her underneath the chin. Her eyes snapped open, looking at me intently as I knelt on the floor beside her bed. "Where?" My voice was a low rumble and her face twisted with an unreadable expression, the shadows playing around on her face, giving her a rather sinister edge.

Bo was a child of no more than six but she was something else as well. The spirit of something lingered inside of her, she held the soul of something *magick*. I knew what it was, it had been explained to me quite clearly. I just disagreed and took her away from the Forests. A child was a child, no matter what lingered underneath her skin.

"They near, bapa. West." Her voice was a low quaver and the shadows disappeared, leaving her that sweet little female I had raised and protected since she had been born. "We leave?" She looked at me, her eyes gleaming at me, pleading with me to say we could stay. I knew what it meant to stay but as I reached out and stroked her cheek with the back of my fingers I gave a grunt and a shake of my head. We would stay for now. I would take care of them.

"Sleep, little one." I got to my feet as she snuggled down into the covers. I would take care of the threat to her as I always had. I left the room quickly, closing the door softly behind me. I didn't bother with my boots as I headed out the front door and into the dark and still night. I headed in the direction given, travelling west, seeking out the scents that would signal my prey.

The beast inside me lifted his head as a musky scent of a were invaded my senses. I bared my teeth, moving faster away from the small home. The rain had washed away our scents by the cabin, I knew that but I also knew the weres were starting to team up with the warlocks to return Bo before the time was up. Those with magick didn't require scents to find us. It made me more and more paranoid. I just hoped BamBam's magick would drown out any attempts to find us. She put off a fair amount of it and I hoped it would confuse any seeking spells.

I shifted my direction, heading towards the were tracking through the forest. I stayed downwind, using it to my advantage as I spotted him through the trees. He had yet to change but there was the familiar angles to his face that let me know his beast was close. I barred my teeth, stilling in my spot as I watched him approach. My beast thrashed against my control, hurling himself at my will. He wanted blood and death. He wanted this scout killed because our little female asked it of us.

The tracker lifted his head, sniffing deeply at the air as he slowly turned around. I seized my chance as he back was partially turned to me and dove out of my hiding spot. I connected with him hard, sending us both crashing to the ground as I let go of control, my beast rising up and to the front to remove the threat that had been tracking us.

My bones cracked and shifted as he pulled forward as we threw hard punches at the tracker. The male let out a heavy snarl, throwing us off, gaining his bearings. My beast burst free from my form, the change painful for me but bearable as he got to his feet, his claws digging into the ground as he sized up his prey. The male looked at us, his eyes flashing yellow as he grinned, licking at the blood that dripped from his nose.

"It's good to see you, Ren. Tell me where she is and I won't have to kill you." We knew this male in the time before Bo. Had been close to us but we cut ties with everyone we had known before. They had chosen us, the strongest of the eastern Forests to watch the small female but they didn't tell me why. When I had learned of what was to happen to her I did as any protector would, I protected.

My beast launched at the male, claws digging deep into the earth to add momentum to his launch. We collided with a force of two mountains, claws ripping and tearing at flesh as teeth sunk deep into muscles and heavy forms rolled and twisted.

My beast knew that the longer the fight drew on the worse the outcome was so when the male took a knee, shifting down, signalling a break between bouts we refused to relent. We stalked towards him, eager to end the threat that dared to approach.

"Have you no honour?" The male spat the question at us as he tried to scramble to his feet, tried to shift in time. We gave no quarter, grabbing his small and delicate human head in clawed hands and slamming it against a tree, driving his face in so hard the tree cracked. We didn't relent, slamming it again and again, growling and snarling as we did so before we took his stomach, digging through his flesh to the organs underneath. Our claws were drawn to his heart, tearing the organ from his body and letting it fall.

I shifted down, my beast entering the confines of my body. Blood cooled on my skin and I held the warm heart in my hand. I looked at it before looking at the male who used to be a friend. I couldn't remember his name now and I didn't care.

"I have honour enough to obey my vow." I lightly tossed the heart at him, watching it roll on the ground, picking up dirt and leaves. "Where is yours?" There was no honour to what he and the others wanted for Bo.

I looked up at the moon hiding behind the clouds, the light called to my beast but he was sated, as was my instinct. We had done as was needed.

We protected.

Chapter Eight
Ease of Magick

Light streaming into the window slowly woke me up. I stretched slowly, my muscles feeling languid and relaxed. I blinked slowly as I let myself practically melt into the bed. My body felt deliciously achy and I reminded of how much I loved the 'day afte'r feeling of having sex. I had been taken for one hell of a ride last night and I was definitely pleased and satisfied after that.

I sat up, attempting to run my hand through my sex mused curls but failed as I hit tangles. I made a slight face as the slight sweaty feeling I had. I might have loved the morning after sex feeling in my muscles but not the after sex feeling on my skin or hair. I wanted a shower.

I stood up, leaving the rumpled bed to fold itself down as my magick ran through me like clockwork. Life was so much simpler when one had magick. I didn't even have to do laundry, everything was done routinely by my magick. I didn't understand how others must have lived doing everything manually.

I grabbed my silk robe from the back of the door and slid it on, the feeling of the silk against my slightly tender skin made me inhale slightly. I pushed the slight stimulation away as best as I could as I tied the sash around my waist. As much as I enjoyed Ren's teeth on my skin it did cause some areas of my body to be over sensitive to contact. I didn't mind it, it was a reminder of him being there and that I enjoyed immensely. It was just distracting.

I padded out of my bedroom, giving a small yawn. The air of the main room smelled of bacon and eggs and I looked around, a shirtless Ren was standing at the stove while Bo was sitting at the table, shovelling food into her mouth as if she would never see it again. She had done the same thing last night as well. I wondered how often she was fed appropriately. I looked down her, studying her, it was clearly not often from how skinny she was.

She looked up at me, her dark eyes gleaming as she gave a smile before she choked. I took a step forward, my heart in my chest right as Ren turned around and thumped her hard on the back. She spat out the food she was choking on and I relaxed as he took her plate from her.

"Slow. Down." The words were clipped and she bared her little teeth at him, a small growl exiting her little chest as she reached for her plate. He gave a returning growl that had her curling forward and submitting underneath his presence. He set her plate back down and she picked up her fork, slowly picking at her food like Ren had ordered.

I walked over, stroking her hair with a smile before I bent down and kissed her forehead. "Sleep well, beauty?" She nodded as she looked up at me, her eyes crinkling at the corners as she chewed her eggs. I once again stroked her hair before I moved towards Ren. I slipped an arm around his waist as I watched him moved bacon around the cast iron pan with a fork. "Where did you get that?" I didn't remember having bacon in my freezer.

He gave a small grunt as he shrugged, his hand landing on my ass as he gave it a rather lazy squeeze. I trailed my nails up his side lightly. "I need to have a shower." I looked up at him as he stiffened slightly. "Care to join me?" He gave another grunt, squeezing my ass cheek once more before giving a rather strained shake of his head.

I gave a small, disappointed sigh. "I'll be in there if you change your mind." I trailed my nails up his side slightly, reaching to trailed one finger over his nipple as he gave a low rumble. "I won't lie, I'll be waiting." I patted his muscular stomach before moving away.

Just being around him was like a straight shot of desire into my veins. I liked that he acted how he wished. He wasn't restrained and I was once again disappointed in myself for not trying out a werewolf before. All that unrestrained passion I had been missing. It was aggravating to realize I had been missing out. As I said before, I was a woman of the flesh and I *adored* physical pleasures, so the fact I hadn't been getting all the pleasure I could was substantially upsetting.

I entered the bathroom, closing the door as the lights came on and the shower started. I untied the robe, shedding it as I moved towards the shower. Steamy air emerged from behind the shower curtain. I pushed it back and stepped into the hot spray. I gave a small moan as the hot spray cascaded over me. I rolled my head, rubbing at my arms and my body to wash away the sweat and sex that lingered on my skin. I trailed my fingers across the red marks that Ren had left across my breasts and inner thighs. I liked seeing them on my pale skin, as he said, it was a reminder to let me know he had been between my thighs.

    I dunked my head underneath the spray, massaging the water into my scalp and doing my best to use the water to help take the tangles out of my hair. When the tangles remained stubborn I reached out with my hand and a hair brush landed in my palm. I flicked my wrist and the brush moved on its own, working out the tangles from the bottom of my hair upwards. I ignored it as I grabbed my body wash and lathered up my wash cloth. I rubbed the sweet smelling soap into my skin and massaged at the achy spots I had in my limbs.

    Once the brush was able to move through my hair freely I held out my hand, the brush settled into my palm and I tucked it onto the shelf I had made sure to have in the shower. I grabbed some shampoo and lathered the red strands, washing them thoroughly. I gave a small groan as I massaged my scalp. No matter what I did, nothing compared to having one's head massaged. I shivered as I rinsed out the shampoo, my hair hair squeaky clean.

    I conditioned my hair, twisting it up into a bun on my head after as I went through the rest of my routine. Thoughts flickered in and out of my head, nothing pressing was truly bothering me. I felt blissfully relaxed and I knew it had everything to do with the sex I had last night. I had sadly forgotten how relaxed it always made me feel afterwards. It left me languid, feeling like soft silk was flowing through my veins.

I knew that I would be entirely upset if Ren told me he wasn't going to slip in my bed any time soon. I knew I might have to hurt him a little to convince him otherwise. Not only was he equipped with the perfect sized cock for the job, he took a rather intriguing pleasure in making sure I was completely and totally satisfied with our frantic and definitely passionate sex.

Not that he needed too. I enjoyed him fucking me just as much as I enjoyed him eating me out, it was just that he had done it without being asked or threatened. *That* was what made it so much better for me.

Desire moved through my veins as I slowly thought about it, my core becoming slick and heated and my nipples budding as my breast grew heavy. I thrust my chest under the spray with a small face. There was no need to get worked up because if Ren was going to join me, he would have done it by now.

I understood why he didn't, Bo was awake and she was young enough to still require being watched. However I acknowledged that any time I thought about Ren it would probably end up with me getting hot and bothered because he had worked me over something good and my body was keyed up because of it.

I rinsed out my hair quickly, no longer wanting to linger because I was going to take far longer than I should have if I did. As delightful as that would have felt I knew it would only serve to frustrate me because it wouldn't be nearly as good as if Ren tended to me. I didn't need him to fuck me more than once to know that.

Once my hair was completely rinsed out I stepped out of the hot shower, the water shutting off as I did so. I grabbed a towel and quickly dried off, trying my hardest to ignore my overly sensitive skin that sent shivers of pleasure through me. It wasn't helping me with not being hot and bothered. I huffed with frustration as I grabbed my robe, slipping it on before towelling my hair mostly dry. I tucked the towel over the curtain rod before leaving the bathroom.

Ren's eyes were immediately on me and I smiled at Bo as she sat on the counter, her little legs dangling as she hummed a strange little tune. I shoved a hand through my hair and headed for my bedroom. I needed to get dressed because we had to head into the city today. Ren had looked at my truck last night and we would pick up the parts he needed to make sure the rust bucket continue to limp along.

I pulled open my lingerie drawer and looked over the various sets that I had and tapped my bottom lip in thought. I still remembered how Ren destroyed my lace black panties and I was still a bit miffed at that. It wasn't like the sets were cheap, I mean I stole them, but that didn't negate the fact they had been worth over a hundred dollars. He had ripped them to shreds. It didn't really matter he had done it to get to my goody jar because he could have just pulled them off.

I became aware there were eyes on me and I crossed my arms over my chest as I tilted my head, baring my neck to the intruder to my room. "Look at all these and I can't choose which one to wear because a certain male has already ruined one set." I tsked lightly and he was soon standing behind me before his arms wrapped around me. One arm wrapping around my waist its hand wiggled underneath my arms to cup a breast as his other one reached down to cup my sex rather possessively.

Desire immediately roared through me, searing my nerves and having my head falling back to his shoulder as his mouth and teeth trailed over my shoulder and neck. "Don't want them ruined. Don't wear them." He stroked my sensitive core over my robe and his talented fingers tweaked my nipple and I helplessly rolled my hips with a small moan.

"But a girl likes to look pretty." My voice was nearly breathless as I ground my ass back against his groin, loving the feeling of his shaft as it pulsed against me through his jeans.

He gave a noncommittal grunt before he nipped at my neck, laving the spot with his tongue. "Females and their baubles and silks." He gave a small huff and I looked forward, watching him move behind me in the mirror, his eyes flicked forward, catching mine. I watched his eyes flashed a golden yellow, the animalistic gleam heavy and present in his gaze. "How did the witch like being fucked by a hated werewolf?" There was a flash of amusement to his eyes and I reached up, running my hand through his hair as I scratched at his scalp.

"She *loved* it." I turned my head, breaking eye contact with him as I looked up at him. "And she would love it again." His chest rumbled as he looked at me. "And again..." I tugged his head down, my lips brushing his. "And *again*." I gave a throaty chuckle at the distressed sound he made as his grip became more possessive before he captured my lips roughly with his own. His tongue thrust into my mouth as his hand move hard and almost frantically between my legs that had equally frantic moans rolling up into my throat as his other hand slipped into my robe, scratching claws against my bare skin before his hot hand cupped my bare breast.

"Bapa?" At the quiet voice we both froze and I slowly pulled away from him, pecking the corner of his mouth before I gently removed his hands from around me. I didn't want to have his touch gone but I knew that we would have very limited time while Bo was awake and running around. I gave Ren a small shove, smirking slightly at the bulge in his jeans as he gave a heavy growl before stalking out of the room.

Despite how my core ached and begged to be satisfied and how I shuddered in agreement to that, I turned back to my dresser. I looked at the sets of lingerie before a small smirk tugged up my mouth as I tried to catch my breath. The male had spoken. I closed the drawer slowly as the smirk deepened.

I would wear none at all.

Chapter Nine
Sweetest Torment

I picked Bo up from her spot where she was holding up her arms, her expression dark with a slight pout. No matter how badly my cock ached and demanded to be satisfied, Bo came first. "What is it, little one?" I wanted to know why she was so upset but she didn't answer and leaned her head against my shoulder as she let out a heavy sigh. "We do not play games." I couldn't help the edge my voice took as I moved towards the stove where I had the plate of bacon.

"Tired." She gave a long and drawn out sigh at that and I jostled her slightly as I shoved a piece of bacon in my mouth. "Why do they keep chasin' us?" There was a sad note to her voice and I jostled her again, moving away from the counter.

I licked the bacon grease off my fingers. "Because they are stupid." So incredibly stupid. They had been stupid when they had placed me as her protector and they were stupid for continuing to chase after us.

"Why?" She made a noise of curiosity as she tucked her head underneath my chin.

"Because I keep killing them." I grinned at that and she let out a small giggle as she pulled back, looking at me before leaning towards me and rubbing her nose on my cheek.

"Hey, hotness, I have a question." At the sinful silk of her voice I looked towards the witch. I nearly choked as I looked her over. She was wearing a tight black crop top, her breasts free from the confines of a bra, her toned and pale stomach showing as runes flickered across her skin and she was wearing pair of jeans that looked damn near painted on.

Feast

My instinct slithered up my spine and I swallowed hard.

The bounty is there

I had never seen a female who looked more like the definition of a male killer than she did in that moment because I swore that if I hadn't already had an aching shaft, seeing that image would have immediately made me shot hard and pass out from lack of blood flow.

She didn't looked at all bothered by my nearly slack jawed reaction as she flicked her red curls over her shoulder. "What was wrong with the truck when you looked?" Her emerald green eyes were lined darker and her lips were painted a fire red and I ground my teeth together, glowering at her.

I did not understand how such a female could live out here alone and dress like that. She looked like temptation personified. "Should be junked." I managed to grunt the words out, doing my best to ignore the pained throbbing in my cock as the witch moved by me, picking up a piece of bacon and eating it slowly, her eyes on me the entire time. The little minx knew exactly what she was doing to me and she was doing it on purpose. My hand ached to redden her perfectly shaped ass.

"Truth *now*." She gave me a small look of warning and she licked her fingers, her tongue swirling around those slim digits with her intent clear with her heated and hooded gaze. I grunted and looked away, jostling Bo slightly, reminding myself of my job.

Bo came first. However it was hard to continually remind myself of that when the female moved close to me, close enough I could smell the sweet scent of her skin. My mouth watered to have my tongue on her flesh once more.

"If you don't tell me, Ren..." Her tone was low and alluring and she reached out, tugging against the waistband of my jeans lightly. She moved closer, going up to her tip toes, her face close enough I could see the flecks of pine green that floated in her irises and feel her warm breath on me chin. "I'm going to fry your balls off of your body and feed them to you." The threat was clear and I snapped my teeth, ready to lay into her when Bo giggled. All my attention diverted to her but she was just giggling as she looked at me.

BamBam's attention was immediately diverted to the small female and she cooed softly reaching for her. I hesitated in passing her over but Bo didn't as she reached for the witch, letting her pull her into her arms as she tapped her nose and cooed to her about how adorable she was. She looked natural with a babe on her hip as she nuzzled Bo's cheek with her nose.

She glanced at me, her eyes darting to my groin as her mouth twitched upwards a fraction. She knew what she was doing to me and I was going to punish her for it, *thoroughly*. "Would you like to go shopping, beauty?" At the question I immediately snapped to attention, my instinct hissing.

Protect

"No." It came out hard and harsh and the female looked at me, her eyebrow quirking before she turned her attention back to Bo, dismissing me entirely. "I said no." Taking Bo anywhere there were a lot of people was dangerous. She was a werefemale, coveted in her rarity, and if anyone got their hands on her she was worth more than her weight in gold.

"I wasn't asking you, Ren. I was asking the little beauty." BamBam's tone didn't change from her soft coo she had been using to speak to Bo and I stood as tall as I could, looking down at the red haired female, doing my best to show her I wasn't to be fucked with. I killed warlocks and witches alike in my protection of my charge and she would join their ranks.

"I said no." A growl rumbled my chest and I narrowed my eyes at her intently. I didn't play games and the female was testing me in one that I refused to play.

"You need to get with the program, honey, because I *am* going shopping and so is the little beauty. She needs some clothes and I need a few things from town." The witch looked at me, her green eyes nearly glowing as her magic sparked that violent amber on her skin. "Understood?" There was an intensity to her gaze that I hadn't been expecting and even my instinct hesitated. There had only been a few witches we had come across in our time that had similar looks and they had been merely level fives. BamBam looked far more powerful than them and I wasn't sure if it was because of the runes on her skin or not.

My instinct fled back into my bones, falling silent as the female's eyes dared me to tell her no. Someone had spoiled her if she demanded her way so violently. I ached to be the one to turn her over their knee and spank her for her attitude but I backed down, inclining my head towards her. Some fights were best left before they started. I didn't know what level of a witch she was and I didn't want to find out while on the receiving end of one of her spells.

"So what was wrong with the truck?" Her mood changed entirely but that small smirk lingered on her mouth that showed her satisfaction with getting me to bow down and I itched to remove it. I could imagine how I would do it and my cock throbbed angrily at me for the images it inspired.

"Fan belts need to be replaced." At my words she gave me a bright smile.

"Well, let's be off. "She gave a firm nod, waving her free hand at the kitchen, everything putting itself away or heading to the sink to be cleaned. As soon as she was satisfied she headed out of the cabin, I followed close behind, my gaze on her flawless form.

I ground my teeth together, doing my best to stop picturing my hands on her curves, on her pert ass as I thrust into her hard for her insolence. Where I would deny her the heights of pleasure she wanted until she submitted beneath me. I knew a female like her would only come to heel through physical and pleasurable torment. I felt a smirk tug up my lips.

How I would *enjoy* putting her in her place.

Chapter Ten
Motherfucking Woman

I walked down the street, Bo tucked against my hip as she played with my hair. I could feel Ren's gaze on me, hot and possessive, just like it had been since I had come out of my bedroom after getting dressed. I wanted to smirk at how easily I had made the male trail after me. I quite enjoyed the feeling. I hadn't felt that sense of power in a very long time.

That and I was feeling very confident. Hell, I was pretty sure I was walking with a bit of a swagger. There was nothing like the ego boost that a great round of sex gave a person.

I jostled Bo slightly and she smiled at me, leaning over and kissing my cheek gently. "Awww, my sweet little beauty." I grinned at her, tapping her nose. "I am going to spoil you rotten!" She smiled before leaned her head on my shoulder.

I wrapped my other arm around her, looking down the street for the magical barrier that would take us to Emporium. Which was just a street... that contained a literal black market. It was a portal of inter-dimensions that took you to whichever shop you wanted, mainly illegal shops or shops that provided you with black curtain, illegal items under the table, but it took you to them.

"So what was it my truck needed?" I looked over my shoulder at Ren and his gaze was clearly on my ass, his focus rather intense and after a moment he blinked.

"Fan belts." It was a low rumble of a voice that had shivers erupting over my skin and naughty thoughts filling my head.

I was actually impressed at his single minded focus he had on my ass. "Do you know what sizes?" He didn't even attempt to speak, just gave a curt nod and I looked forward once again. Humans and fae were crossing the street as I walked down it. Their eyes down and their forms hunched away from our small group. I half wondered if it was because of how I wore my magick or the hulking werewolf that was stalking me.

I fought back a grin at that thought. He was stalking willing prey and it amused me greatly but if he wished to play predator I would let him because I did enjoy being chased. There was no point in being as sexy as I always made myself to look if no one was going to pursue me. True I dressed sexy for myself at times but I wasn't going to lie and say that I didn't also dress like that to watch people's eyes widen or their jaws drop.

A shimmering 'E' appeared in the air above my head and I stopped walking immediately, turning on my heel to look at the brick wall. The Emporium changed locations along the street fairly often. One had to be a creature of magick to know where it was, well not just magick, supernatural. One had to not be human in order to spot it. I glanced at Ren as he stopped beside me, his presence nearly enveloping me with his heat and scent.

His gaze lingered on me and then Bo before he jerked his head at the wall. "Marketplace." With that word he pushed through the wall, not at all fazed by the magick that surrounded him. I watched after him for a moment before I shrugged.

"Marketplace it is, Bo-peep." I tapped her nose and pushed through the portal. There was a swooshing feeling in my stomach as I stepped through to the other side. Cobblestones materialized underfoot as we stepped through the entrance to the market place.

Bo gave a small whine of discomfort that I tsked at. Poor thing, it must have been her first portal. "Bapa!" At the name she was plucked out of my arms and held to Ren's large chest as he shushed her, his expression dark and foreboding to all those that milled around. She wrapped her arms around his neck and he held her gently. A part of me melted as I watched him with her. It was clear he had a great affection for her and he would protect her no matter not.

Different coloured faes moved around with their head down, avoiding looking at us. I looked around, my eyes landing on a door with a sign showing a crow on its back over it.

I glanced at Ren before looking back at the door. "I'm heading to the Broken Crow." I didn't wait for his reply as I strode towards the door. I couldn't stand around. I was banished and that technically meant the Emporium was off limits to me.

I shoved the door open, aware that Ren was close behind me as I stepped into the dim store, a series of bells ringing across the ceiling as I did so. A witch dressed in gauzy material practically floated out into view and she froze in place as I grinned at her.

"Hello, Violet."

Her face paled as I moved towards her. "Miranda, you aren't supposed to be here." Her voice was a nearly breathless hiss as her eyes darted around frantically before they narrowed at me.

I shrugged my shoulders, tapping my fingers against the dusty products on the shelves. "Why not? I have to pick up a few things." Just a few little things to make some adjustments to my cabin. I did have guests and all that. Preparations needed to be done in order for my cabin to function as it should.

She inhaled deeply as her eyes widened slightly. "You need to leave. *Right now.*" She walked over and reached for me when Ren let out a heavy growl. Violet gave a startled yelp and jumped backwards. "You brought a *werewolf* into my shop?" Her eyes widened further as she stared at me.

I widened my own eyes with a sharp gasp. "*Werewolf? Where?*" I whirled around and winked at Ren before he narrowed his eyes and moved to the other side of the shop, Bo settled in his arms against his chest. I slowly turned to look at Violet. "I have no clue what you are talking about, Violet." I blinked at her slowly and she had her eyes trained on Ren and I didn't need to be a were to practically smell the wary fear that radiated off of her.

Her gaze snapped to me and she grabbed my around the arm, practically dragging me to the back of the store. I allowed the action, knowing it was better to let her blow her steam out where Ren would be a bit further away if he took offence. "What the *hell* are you doing?" Her grip was tight on my arm and I flicked it off.

"Shopping. I thought that was obvious." I gestured to the store, watching as her face went more and more red. Violet wasn't banished per-say but she was stuck running Broken Crow because she owed an Elder a hefty debt. Rumour had it she was stuck to Elder Irma, a heinous bitch of a witch. I didn't know if it was true and I didn't care enough to ask.

"Don't play dumb!" The words were a lowered hiss of agitated fear and she pointed at Ren as subtly as she could. "Why the hell are you hanging out with a couple of werewolves? Do you know what would happen to you, to *me*, if they are caught in here?" I looked at Ren slowly, letting my gaze roam over his defined body. Even in a t-shirt I could see the muscles he held under his skin. He truly was a *fine* ass male.

I slowly turned to blink at Violet. "I still don't see what you are talking about." I knew that me denying Ren was even in the store was driving her nuts and I enjoyed that it was. I liked fucking with witches. Last time I had let loose a group of pixies into her store. She had screamed at me for it and I had simply pretended I had no clue what she was talking about and that I couldn't see the little green flying creatures knocking shit off her shelves.

Her expression twisted into irritation and my amusement ratcheted up a fair bit. "*Seriously*, Miranda?"

I made a face at my real name. "BamBam." I had changed it for a reason and everyone else needed to get with the program.

"I am not using that absurd nickname." She made a sound of disgust and I rolled my eyes at her slight theatrics. "Do you understand the implications of what you are engaging in? You are banished but they can still burn you for this! They can burn me for even allowing them into the store!" Her voice pitched upwards in panic and I rolled my eyes. She was always so dramatic and I honestly didn't want to deal with her panicked fear. Witches were all so stuffy.

"I need ten grams of earth of the damned, twelve millilitres of mermaid tears, and a phoenix brush." I watched as she froze at my request before her expression turned blank but no matter how she tried to hide it, her eyes kept shifting.

"I run a legitimate business, Miranda. I cannot, nor would I, sell them to anyone below an Elder status. You know this." Each word was carefully said in a precise way that let me know she was one again repeating what had been told to her.

"I know you are just being stingy. I want it or some Elders are going to find out you sell some pretty mind altering chemicals out your back door. Love potions?" I tsked and she clenched her jaw tightly, her eyes narrowing to slits.

"You have no proof!" At that I wanted to grin. Violet was always so easy to push. I would have had troubles if she kept clean but she liked the gold too much to quit her side business. I almost wanted to ask her why she wanted the gold that much, she never went out anywhere, but I honestly didn't care.

"We go through this song and dance every single time, Violet. You always give in." It was just a matter of time before she did. She went over the same things again and again and it never ended with me backing down. A bit of force always worked well in my favour when it came to her.

"If I sel you anything that only an Elder can use, Elder-"

"I don't care about what will happen to you." hat was a pure truth. I honestly didn't care what happened to her. She would give me what she wanted and if she wanted things to be okay outside of that, she just needed to use her magick. "Give me what I need and I will be out of your hair and your pathetic little shop."

She swallowed hard before her jaw lifted in a stubborn position and I felt agitation roll through me as she refused to back down. "If you turn me into the Elders I will turn you in for fraternizing with a werewolf." Her unrepentant look was all it took.

I snapped my hand out, grabbing her throat as I sent my magick to punish her for her insolence. She hit her knees, gasping for air as my magick shoved hers out of her body, slowly overtaking her very core. I could rip her magick from her body and take it for my own and she knew that.

"I will tell!" She gasped it out and I bent down close to her face.

"I will leave you magickless and penniless. Nothing but amusement keeps me from robbing you blind and simply taking what I want or need." I tightened my grip and her face was growing a little grey as her eyes nearly bugged out, her lips turning a dark blue as she struggled to breathe as I forced my magick deeper into her. "You *amuse* me, Violet, don't stop amusing me." I titled my head as she nearly withered before me.

"Don't test me, Violet. You won't like it." I had no feelings for her, I could force her to become a dried out husk and I would feel nothing for it. She reached for me, her eyes twitching, pleading with me to let her go. I yanked my magic back and she gasped, choking on the air as colour rapidly returned to her face. "Lesson learned?" I crouched down beside her and she rubbed at her throat, taking in deep and wheezing breaths.

"Get my shit and don't you *ever* fucking threaten me again." I stood up, watching her as she knelt on the floor. I didn't like it when paltry little parlour magick trick witches decided to threaten me. She was a bug I could crush beneath my heel if I so desired it and she needed to *never* forget that.

She looked at me warily. "I won't forget this." Her voice was raspy as she managed to get to her feet, her legs shaking, looking like they didn't want to hold her weight up.

"I hope so, if you did that negates the lesson I just taught you." I waved her off. "Also some fan belts for my truck, you know the model and year, and some cute clothes for a six year old girl." She gave me a dark look but disappeared into the back room to get me what I wanted, rubbing her throat as she did so.

I headed towards where Ren and Bo were looking through heavy winter jackets, the dusty that flew off of them as Ren shoved them across the bar was almost enough to choke a horse and I waved my hand in front of my face, giving a small cough.

"She's just getting all my shit and then we can head back to the cabin." Ren glanced down at me and gave a noncommittal shrug. I moved closer, sliding my hand across his lower back. "We can have some fun afterwards if you want." At my breathless words his attention was immediately back on me, his gaze deep and probing as it mt mine. I let him see just what he wanted. I wanted him to see the desire I had for him to push me up the closest surface and entered me hard and fast.

He bent down, trailing his lips across my cheek before nipping at my jaw and moving towards my ear. He trailed his teeth across the sensitive shell and I shuddered as he let out a little rumble of enjoyment at my reaction. Sadly I had to pull away as Bo skipped over, a wide grin on her face as she held her arms up at Ren.

"Up, Bapa." It was a short little demand but Ren said nothing as he dutifully picked her up. I looked between the two of them. I knew there was something going on and I didn't like being out of the loop, at all.

Still I pushed it away before I went up on my tiptoes, pecking Ren's cheek before nuzzling his ear with my nose. "I'm wearing the lingerie you picked out." At the heated whisper I felt him stiffen rapidly before I flounced off.

Violet came out from the back room, a plain brown box in her arms that more than likely held everything I needed. She glowered at me and I gave her a grin in return as I picked up the box and headed to the entrance. I swayed my hips a bit more, exaggerating the movement because I could feel Ren's piercing gaze on my ass.

A low rumble escaped him as he followed me out of the door and my grin widened because I knew the reason he was staring so intently and that was because both Ren and I knew he picked out no lingerie at all.

Chapter Eleven
Know When to Fold Them

I scowled at the oily engine, trying hard to get the fan belt back on. My hand slipped and my knuckles bashed against the engine block. I cursed at the pain and Bo giggled. "Need help, bapa?" She patted my back and I held out my throbbing hand. She grabbed it and kissed the back of it before patting it gently.

"Much better, little one." I grinned as she gave another giggle, letting my hand go. I wiggled my fingers at her, "Pass me the screwdriver." There were a few moments before I felt the screw driver being placed on my hand. I pulled my hand back down to where I was holding the fan belt before I wiggled the screw driver into place, grunting as I twisted the roller. The piece of shit refused to move and I wiggled the screwdriver back and forth, in my attempt to get the belt back on the roller.

Bo drummed her little hands on my back as she hummed happily and I couldn't shake the grin of my face. I liked it when my little female was pleased enough to hum. She didn't do it enough while on the run. I disliked how I had to take her from her room of pink and purple silks and satin cushions and into the cold and unforgiving wilds. I knew it was for her safety but it didn't stop my inherent guilt at my inability to make sure she was comfortable and safe.

"I like Bam." At the excited words she grabbed my shirt, yanking at it frantically.

"The little witchling is amusing." I gave another grunt as I finally managed to get the roller to spin and the belt to slide into place. Bo continued to pull at my shirt, grunting herself with her frustration. I brushed her hands off as stood up, my back cracking from being bent over for so long and I looked at the little female. She was dressed in a pink sundress that BamBam had gotten for her, her hair in messy pigtails as she grinned at me from her spot on the front of the truck.

"She's fun!" She launched at me and I caught her with ease, holding her against my hip as I closed the hood of the truck. It was still a piece of shit but at least it wasn't in danger of imminently dying.

"She's something." She was hot, wicked, and a tease. Just the reminder of her was starting to stir my cock back up to full attention after I had spent so long getting it to settle down as I worked on the truck. It didn't help that all I could picture was pulling down those jeans and seeing her bare before me.

The cabin door flew open and the female in question came barrelling out, her chest heaving and her eyes wide. "We have unwanteds inbound. Get your ass in the house!" I didn't even question her words, running for the open door with her close behind. Bo's safety was paramount to everything and once she was safe I would protect her as I was supposed to. I slowed down as I got inside and BamBam shoved at my back, pushing me towards her bedroom. "Need to shut down the portals, my bedroom is the only real room in the house." I gave a heavy growl, unable to help myself at the threats that had been announced.

I headed straight for the room, aware of the witch right behind me but the moment I got into the room she slammed the door closed behind me. I set Bo down and tried to open the door, a force repelled me back.

"Sorry, sexy, but I gotta do as I do and you dying is not in my cards right now." Her voice was muffled and I bared my teeth and threw myself at the wooden door but was violently thrown backwards. The magick sent me stumbling away from any of BamBam's things and I gave a heavy snarl that made Bo whimper.

I took another run at the door and was once again thrown onto my ass. I got to my feet and Bo scrambled onto BamBam's bed, hiding underneath the covers. I shook my head rapidly moving closer to the door, testing out how close I could get before the magick would send me back. I came within inches but the moment I reached for the handle I was shoved away.

I bared my teeth as I could hear movement on the other side. Two sets of footsteps could be heard and I could smell the were immediately.

Protect

My instinct roared at me, sinking hard into my bones and my muscles as it called my beast up but I did my best to fight them both off. I knew I was unable to do anything, BamBam had somehow magickally locked me in and I would only come out if she wanted me out. I bared my teeth at that.

I *needed* to protect!

"Nice place you have, Miranda." It was a cold and sharp voice despite the feminine edges it had and I knew it must have been a witch. They were getting closer. Bo and I couldn't stay if they were able to track us down.

"I make do. What the hell are you doing here, Florence?" There was a heavy bite of hate to BamBam's voice that nearly surprised me. It was clear she must not have had a very good relationship with the witch. It was surprising because I knew witches stuck together.

"Stopping by... making sure you aren't doing anything that will get you... *burned.*" Even I could hear the disgust in her voice as she said it and I ground my teeth together hard, my jaw aching from the force of it.

"I'm not within your rules anymore, Florence. You made sure I knew that when you had me banished." Realization dawned on me, BamBam hated the female for banishing her and I rested my hand beside the door, hanging my head, closing my eyes as I focused hard. I knew the were was there but I couldn't hear him, he wasn't moving. I didn't like the situation, I didn't like being trapped.

"Violet said you ransacked her shop with two werewolves. A large male and a child." Apprehension prickled over my entire body. I knew going to the city was a bad thing. That witch had told and now Bo was in danger. I had a sudden urge to find her and coat my teeth and skin with her blood. I bared my teeth, a low growl rumbling my chest.

"Oh please, you are going to believe that drugged up tramp?" Venom coated BamBam's tone heavily. "That little bitch will wished I had ransacked her place when I get through with her." I could almost guarantee that the little witchling had the same murderous urge as I did. I doubted the witch named Violet would live past the week.

Large footsteps started to move around and I resisted the urge to hit the door, knowing it would only send me flying back, making me miss the conversation. I needed to know what was going on.

"You know fraternizing with werewolves are *illegal.*" There was an edge of glee to the other witch's words as the were gave a heavy grunt, moving towards the bedroom door.

"Says you with *dumbass* there." At BamBam's voice the footsteps stopped and he gave a heavy growl. I ground my teeth together to not shout at the witchling to not rile the male up. He smelled of violence and she didn't know what he could do. "*Shut it*, fido. If you were smart you would give this one a stiff fucking and maybe, just *maybe*, that would remove the giant fucking stick she has shoved up her ass." A thick silence fell and my own eyes widened at that.

"*Excuse me?*" The witch's voice was low and there was a deep rumble from the were that had me on edge.

"You fucking heard me, Florence." BamBam's tone was hard and sharp. "So did you." The Rumble turned into a snarl and I tightened my hands into fists, trying my hardest to not listen to my instinct as it swirled around, hissing at me to claw the door open and protect the mouthy female. "I suggest you bend her over and give her a good, long, and hard fucking. It would do the world a fucking favour." Silence fell once more before there was a loud snarl that had me tensing and the sound of a crash.

"That all you got?" At BamBam's shouted response I shoved at the door. I was flung backwards but I tried again, and again, and again. I could hear the sounds of screams and bangs, snarling and growling, through the door as the fight continued.

The little witchling was getting hurt trying to protect me and Bo. I needed to help her. My heart thudded in my chest and head as I slammed into the magickal barrier again and again in my frantic attempts to reach her. My shoulder popped out of place, the pain fleeting as the next slam shoved it back into place. The sounds behind the door grew more and more frantic and I snapped and snarled, fighting my hardest to reach her as there was a sudden scream and the wet sound of blood splashing against walls and then utter silence.

It seemed to radiate out of every inch of space and I let out a roar of anger as I slammed into the door. It buckled and flew open underneath the force of my body colliding with it. My heart lurched, the magick was gone and that meant either BamBam had let me out or she was dead. I looked around, blood and gore coated the walls and bits of flesh hung from the ceiling. I took in the room before my eyes landed on the red haired witch as she wiped at her bleeding nose and mouth.

"Where are they?" The words came out garbled and her intense eyes were on me, silently watching.

Be wary

My instinct slithered up my spine, touching every nerve as it did so. My nerves prickled with awareness and the hair on the back of my neck stood up as I looked at her. It was clear she was in pain, it was how she held her ribs, how she stood, but not a single flicker of pain showed on her face.

Danger lies in wait

She tilted her head before giving a cold and lazy smile that prickled at my nerves even worse. "Everywhere."

Underestimated her

My instinct squeezed my chest as I slowly looked around, now seeing the tufts of were fur that were plastered on the wall amid the viscera. She had killed them... *both* of them. Exploded them without warning or words. I had never seen a witch with enough power to do that.

I looked back at her and that smile disappeared entirely, her face sharpening to a rather dangerous degree as magick swirled around her violently. I took a half step back and she bared her teeth in a parody of the grin and snapped them together with a sound that had me shuddering.

"You need to tell me what is going on and you need to tell me now." The words were said low but they carried the weight of the promise of death they held if I were to lie to her.

Female is dangerous

The word was whispered in my ear, my instinct squeezing my gut tightly with wary apprehension as I looked at her nearly glowing eyes.

Female is deadly

Chapter Twelve
Brain Bleach Needed

I stared at the weremale. He looked apprehensive, shifting on his feet as his eyes darted about. I dared him to try and downplay what the hell was going on. I heard bits and pieces from the minds of the two slushies that now coated my cabin's walls. They had been looking for Ren and Bo and I wanted to know why I got the shit kicked out of me for it.

"They want Bo." That was more than fucking obvious.

I kissed my teeth, narrowing my eyes as my magick ran wild through my veins. It was like bees buzzing with its agitation and Ren really didn't want to be at the end of that agitation. "*Why?*" It was a harsh and clipped word and Ren's jaw clenched, the muscles ticking rapidly.

"To stop the curse." He looked at me but stopped speaking. I gave a small but jerky gesture for him to continue, hiding the wince I got as my ribs rubbed together. That were was fucking lucky I didn't have the restraint to not kill him because I would have ripped his testicles out through his throat for that fucking move. He threw me into the fucking cupboards.

"I don't-"

"You don't want to fucking test me right now, Ren." My magick's buzz turned sharper and I bared my teeth as it nearly rattled my skull. "*Tell. Me.*" There was a downside to working your magick through your body and that was you were subject to its moods and right now my magick was fucking pissed and wanted an outlet.

"They wanted to do a confinement spell using seven warlocks and Bo to seal the curse in an unmarked grave for the rest of eternity." It was the most verbal I had ever heard him and the most eloquent. Usually he was all grunts but apparently he could form *actual* sentences. "They believe The End Bringer's soul resides within her."

At the unfamiliar name I gave another gesture. "End Bringer being?"

"Rowenya." He stared at me, his muscles tense as if he were waiting for me to make the next move.

That made sense. Didn't stop them from being utterly fucking stupid but it made sense. "Got it." I rolled my head, openly wincing at the pain as my magick's anger settled to a simmer. So some stupid assholes decided to do a containment spell on a little girl. I gave a small shudder.

"You know what they plan to do?" Ren asked it warily as he moved a fraction closer, stopping right before rather long strip of... *something* fell from the ceiling in front of him.

"Yup." I did and it was fucking disgusting and all kinds of wrong.

"I know they plan to bury her alive but I do not understand what a containment spell is." Ren looked at me, his eyes gleaming in the light and I shifted on my feet, nearly doubling over at the stabbing pain I felt. I was pretty sure the were tore into me with his fucking claws.

"Basically it's taking the caster of the curse and forcing the spell back into them." I looked at him, gauging his expression. I knew Bo wasn't his child but he took care of her as if she was everything to him, as if he would never let the bad of the world touch her. I knew he wasn't going to like what I was going to say but I gave a heavy sigh.

Tit for tat, he shared and now I had to. "As the spell was... sexual in nature, due to the conception part of it, the only way to force it back into the castor is to...you know..." I trailed off. I really didn't want to say it. I felt dirty that it even came into my head. Bo was a little girl and they were going to force that onto her with seven fucking warlocks before burying her alive? That was all sorts of stupid and fucked up.

I watched as confusion flickered in his eyes as they narrowed. I could see him thinking about it, trying to put the pieces together before his eyes flashed a bright yellow and he gave a heavy snarl, his form bulging and twisting with his anger. A heavy rumbled shuddered the air and I blinked, watching as he nearly shifted, garbled sounds emerging from his throat and fur pushing out of his pores.

I slowly shook my head before holding out my hand, my magick pulsating before I flung my hand behind me. The witch and were slushy I made on the walls was immediately cleared from the room and sent out the front door. I flicked my hand at Ren, my magick shoving him against the wall and holding him there as his shift was stopped completely. "Beauty, where ever you are. *Don't. Move.*" I knew this was going to hurt like a motherfucker but I had to do it.

Ren thrashed in my magick's hold and I bared my teeth, gritting them at the pain as I shifted on my feet to look at him. "Enough." I didn't need any distractions for what I was going to do next. Once he fell still I let him go and swirled my hands, the earth of the damned lines I had laid down appeared, lifting into the air. The runes I had painted onto the walls with the phoenix feather paintbrush shone a brilliant blue as they lifted off the wooden walls, hovering in the air.

I closed my eyes, letting myself go relaxed as best as I could with the wounds I had as I let my magick flow through me. It wasn't smooth and it was jerky as it flowed around the broken bones and wounds on my skin, the jerkiness of my magick made me grit my teeth as it highlighted the pain my body was in. I took a deep breath. This was something I was definitely going to feel in the morning.

I held my hands out from my sides, palms up, letting the spell fall from my lips. It was pulled from me rapidly as the runes and designs swirling around and around. I felt my body lift off the ground as I extended the magick further, encasing the cabin and reaching even further to the truck despite how the pain made me want to throw up. I could feel the build up and the tension as it thrummed my muscles painfully from where I had taken blows.

Sweat beaded on my forehead as my body screamed its pain at me. I held on as long as I could, never faltering in the spell as I felt the jump portal start to pull us in before, like the snap of a rubber band stretched too far, we were yanked through. I hit the ground as the magick instantly dissipated, my breaths coming in wheezes as tears burned my eyes. I curled up slightly, my limbs shaking as the pain roared through me in its angry intensity.

Hands grasped at me, pulling me close and I pushed Ren away, my hands and arms shaky. I shook my head. "I'm fine." I tried to stand up but my arms gave out and I gave a rather pitiful cry that I wanted to slap myself for as my ribs ground together in my chest.

A dark rumble filled Ren's chest as he gathered me close to his chest before standing up. "Shut up, witchling." It was a heavy order and I felt the corner of my mouth lift slightly.

"I don't need a hero, Ren." I didn't. I could pull myself together in a few hours. I just needed rest.

"Good cause I'm not one." I looked up at him at the words and his eyes bore into mine, the darkness all encompassing as the heat of his body sunk into me, mixing with the pain. I blinked, the movement slow as I winced heavily, a surge of pain rolling through me with the grace of a freight train. I said nothing else as I leaned my head against his shoulder with a slight whimper.

I wished I hadn't slushied that were because I would have loved to make him feel every ache and pain I currently felt. My ribs ground together as Ren shifted his arms around me and my breath caught in my chest at the pain. I frowned, closing my eyes tightly. The were might have been dead but Violet wasn't and would have made that little pay for it ten fold. A tiny smile tugged my lips up at the thought. She would wish she hadn't fucked me over by the time I got through with her and that thought was *almost* worth the pain.

Chapter Thirteen
No Cure

The female sunk towards me. I could hear her teeth grinding and I carried her to the bathroom. After whatever magick she did, the doors had once again appeared. Her body shook and I bared my teeth at it. She was hurt and it was because she protected me and Bo. I snapped my teeth together as I set her down beside the tub, turning on the water quickly before turning back to her and reaching for her shirt.

She lightly slapped my hands away, her eyes narrowing. "I'm not a child, I can do it myself." I ignored her weak slaps and sliced her shirt off with my claws. I bared my teeth and growled at the purple and black bruising that encased the right side of her torso heavily. I grabbed her arms, looking her over. A dark rumble exited my beast and shook my bones as I saw the deep claw marks the were had left on her back. They had been bleeding but they weren't anymore and I wondered if it was due to her magick.

I carefully lifted her off of the floor and her legs trembled and her form was nearly limp as I undid the button of her jeans. I held her steady as I used one hand to push the material over her hips. She made a pained sound, leaning on me heavily as I shoved the jeans down until she could step out of them herself.

"Bapa?" At the wavering voice I turned my head, Bo was standing in the doorway and I looked down at BamBam.

"Help her. I'm fine." She waved me off, attempting to stand on her own, her face pale and ashy with the pain. I didn't believe her for a moment but I slowly let my arm drop and headed for Bo. I picked her up, glancing over my shoulder as the witchling sat heavily on the side of the tub, holding her ribs with her arm as her other hand griped the edge of the tub so hard her knuckles were white.

"What happened?" Bo's vice was small and wavering as I carried her out of the bathroom and towards the bedroom BamBam had created for her.

"She fought with a were." She had killed him but he still put his hands on her, still marked her skin and harmed her. The beast inside me was unsettled by that, angry and restless. He wished to hurt something, kill anything because we had been stuck, denied helping the female, denied our ability to protect her.

Bo gave a small gasp as I set her down on her bed. "Oh no." Her little face looked stricken and I chucked her chin lightly.

"She's tough. Be fine." I couldn't really look into Bo's eyes and not experience mind numbing rage at the thought of what awaited her at the hands of those who sought us. I thought burying her alive was bad enough but to defile her in such a way before hand? Survival of the species or not, no cure would ever require such a heinous act.

"I wanna help." She moved to get off the bed and I grabbed her around the waist before tugging up her dress.

"You are going to go to sleep." I pulled the dress off of her, laying it at the foot of the bed as I tucked her into the bed, pulling the blankets over her.

Her bottom lip stuck out, trembling as her eyes glimmered with tears. "I wanna help." It was a forlorn set of words but I shook my head.

"You do not need to see such things, little one." I wanted to keep her from the horrors of what would happen to those who defied the Order of the Forests. I didn't want her to see the witchling harmed as she was. "I need you to sleep, to think of this no more. The witchling will be alright and will be better tomorrow." At least I hoped she would. I didn't know what I would do if she was down and out for a while. I was positive her magick would help her heal.

"Promise?" Her dark eyes gleamed at me, the tiny beast inside of her stirring with her high emotions and I gave a slow nod before pending down and pressing my lips to her forehead and brushing my thumb across her cheek.

The thought that some saw her as a means to an end was a fist to the stomach, it was a burning in my veins that I knew I could never scratch out. The Forests wanted her, not for her sex or the spark of a magick soul within her, but for something so vile and cruel I could not understand why they would continue to follow and believe the words spoken to them by the High Kings. There was a wrongness in their demands and I did not understand how some could not see it as I did.

"Sleep, my little one. All will be well in the morning." I smoothed her hair back before I straightened and left the room, closing the door quietly behind me. I moved into the bathroom and BamBam had already settled herself into the bath, her head leaning against the edge of the tub as she sat mostly curled up. I could see her body shaking and I shut the door before pulling off my shirt and shedding my pants.

Her emerald green eyes flicked to me and a faint smile turned up the corners of her mouth as I moved closer. "Such a tease. Showing me the goodies when I'm in no condition to appreciate them." She gave a muffled groan as she sat up straight. I gave a small grunt, not answering her as I stepped into the bath with her, sitting down behind her before I grabbed her carefully and brought her to my chest. "When I am feeling better I am going to demand *this* immediately." She grasped my semi-hard cock in her hot hand and gave a light squeeze.

I fought back a groan at the feeling of her hand on me and gently moved it off of my cock. "No touching." Desire made my voice rough and I could feel my shaft pulsing in angry desire. It had been awoken and wanted to be satisfied but her for was too delicate for such a breeding.

"You're no fun." Her tone was pouting and I could imagine her full bottom lips sticking out in a tantalizing fashion as I grabbed the washcloth and gently started to clean her skin of the blood that was tacky on her form. She let out a faint hiss of pain as I cleaned around the deep gashes the were left on her.

I snapped my teeth together, a growl vibrating the air as I left my throat. "Stupid female. Taking on a were." She didn't need to be putting herself in danger like that. I didn't want her harmed, her marked up like she was.

"The fact I am alive and he is dead pretty much shows he was the stupid one for taking on me." There was a faint edge of gloating to her tone and I couldn't help but tsk as I gently moved the cloth across her shoulders. I lifted my knees, lifting her arms as I did so. She hissed at that, leaning to the right as if that would protect her broken ribs.

"You are hurt." Fairly badly. Not that she would die but she would be in pain for a substantial amount of time. I did not like seeing those brutal wounds on her.

She gave a heavy scoff at my words. "And he is dead. I think mine trumps his."

I trailed the cloth down her arm, gripping at the slim appendage with my hand, massaging her muscles. "Why don't you heal?" She hadn't once looked like she was going to do so. It was bothersome. I knew witches had the ability.

"Because I'm tapped out right now." She let out a faint sigh as I abandoned the cloth as I slid my fingers between hers.

I captured her hand in mine and brought it up, looking at her smooth skin. There were no runes flashing anywhere on her body. "I don't understand." I didn't realize there were limits on a witch's ability. I hadn't really been taught much abut them and I wondered if that was for a reason. The less we knew about them the less we would try to engage them.

"Just because I have the equivalent of the power of the sun behind me doesn't mean I don't get tired after doing big magick." She gave a heavy sigh, leaning back against me slightly, mindful of her ribs and the claw marks.

I lazily wrapped my arms around her, resting my chin on her head. "What spell?" The sight of her eyes glowing, her runes flashing as the cabin trembled and the air warped around her has been equal parts enthralling and terrifying. I had never seen magick like that before.

"I teleported the cabin and the truck." Her words were murmured and I narrowed my eyes slightly.

"Why?" The magick she used seemed unnecessary. She had killed the witch and the were were dead, she killed them. That would have bought her time to heal and do her spell the day after that but she had done the spell even with knowing she would be 'tapped out'. She was such a strange creature.

"I knew Violet was going to rat me out." At the name I let out a heavy growl. That witch would pay for what she had done. BamBam waved me off slightly. "I knew I would have to do it to escape the jackasses chasing you and me. They had my location and that meant more would come." I paused, processing her information and then gave a short nod. It made sense and she had made the right decision but that didn't mean I had to enjoy it.

"Ahh... the witch and the were... you... they were..." I didn't know how to put it into words. She had done something to them to render them into the paste like state they had been in when I came out of the bedroom.

"I exploded them. My magick has a tendency of doing that when I get pissed." She said it so easily but I tucked the knowledge away for use later but the message was clear. Keep the witchling happy. "It was why I was banished. I exploded a witch because she came at me for fucking her warlock and accidentally did it without the appropriate tools."

She made a sound of disgust in her throat. "He was a fucking terrible lay so I was pissed that I got banished because of him." I couldn't keep the chuckles in as I heard that. I took great pleasure in knowing I was better than such a male. She had a warlock set his eyes on her but she derided his ability to please his female and was agitated for being banished for such a poor male but she had praised me heavily for my performance, demanding more from me.

I shifted my head, trailing my teeth across the shell of her ear as my cock hardened to the point of pain. I wouldn't mind another round with her, as soon as possible at that as well.

She made a faint sound, wiggling in my lap. "Stop teasing. Pressing that cock of yours against me and all but telling me to enjoy it when I can't." There was an edge of petulance to her voice and I smirked, nipping at her ear lobe gently before I slowly stood up. I bent down, picking her up and cradling her to my chest before I stepped out of the bath.

She gave a slow and lazy wave of her hand and I could hear the tub draining. She slumped against me after that, her breathing coming out slightly wheezed. "Alright, *now* I'm tapped out." She pressed her head against my shoulder, shoving her forehead against my neck as she gave a small whimper.

I carried her to her bedroom, slowly setting her on the bed where the covers were shoved back. She looked exhausted and I knew she would need help to help heal herself from her ordeal. A pale and slim hand gripped my wrist as I tugged the blankets over her form. I looked at her and she blinked slowly. "A containment spell wouldn't work on her, Ren." Her eyelids were droopy with exhaustion and I narrowed my own at her.

"What do you mean?" If they were mistaken in their prophecy, in their plan, then Bo was safe.

"They need Rowenya's soul or her blood and they have neither." Her eyes closed slowly. "Stupid jackasses would defile a little girl for no reason because there is no cure for what Rowenya did." Her voice trailed off and I wanted to ask her what she meant but she was already asleep.

I paused for a moment before moving onto the bed beside her, laying on my side next to her, wrapping my arm around her side gently as I held her close. I would ask the witchling what she meant when she woke up but right now I would protect her as she had done for me.

Chapter Fourteen
Unmaking

I woke up to a deep burning ache that rolled through my entire body. The only sound I was able to make was a pained whimper as I tried to move only to have the burning turn into a ferocious searing. I felt like I had been hit by a fucking freight train travelling at two hundred miles an hour. I inhaled sharply, scolding myself heavily. I knew I was going to feel it in the morning and I had to buck up and be a big girl about it.

My breath came in slight pants as I rolled over, putting my feet over the edge of the bed, attempting to get up. A heavy growl was all the warning I had before I was scooped up and deposited back on the bed gently.

"Stay." Ren's voice was a low rumble before he turned away, muttering something about me being stubborn as he grabbed a glass of water from my beside table. He looked haggard and tired and I couldn't help how my mouth twitched upwards at his appearance.

"You not sleep any, fido?" I needed something to help me forget the pain I was in and teasing Ren seemed to be the perfect solution. He ignored the question as he gently cupped the back of my head, lifting it up slightly and pressing the cup to my lips. I drank rather greedily, surprised at just how thirsty I was. He pulled the cup away and slowly lowered my head back down to the pillow. "Looks like you can be domesticated, wolf man." He grunted in response to my words and I winced as I shifted on the bed, my ribs hurt like a son of a bitch.

He set the glass on the bedside table and I looked towards the bedroom door, frowning slightly. "Where's my little Bo-peep?" I was a little concerned and wanted to see how she fared with the teleportation.

"Napping." His response was short and I shifted on the bed, panting slightly as I attempted to sit up.

Ren shoved my shoulders back down to the bed, a deep rumble exiting his chest as he looked down at me. "As long as you are under my care, you aren't leaving this bed." He said the words low and I was suddenly aware of the heat of his hands and his strength as he essentially pinned me down.

I stared up at him, tracing his features with my eyes, his strong jaw, his dark eyes, and slightly crooked nose that let me know he was one hell of a bruiser.

Gods was he sexy.

I was a little pissed off because I was a little bit too down and out to do anything about it. "Alright. No leaving the bed on your watch." I slowly relaxed into the bed, watching his stern mouth relax a fraction, the one corner twitching upwards as if he were pleased by my sudden docility.

He slowly removed his hands and I let out a playfully heaving sigh, my bottom lip sticking out. I much rather preferred to have his hands on me. "Can you get me some quartz from my chest the kitchen?" He gave me a rather narrowed eyed look of suspicion before I shifted my head, wincing as I did so as my muscles seemed to protest even the smallest movements. "It's a healing stone and if I am going to take care of the worst of the wounds I'm going to need all the help I can get." At that he gave a slow nod, leaving the room.

I watched him before quickly waving my hand, my magick flaring to life as the door slammed shut behind him. I could hear him give out a snarl of displeasure before the door shuddered as he slammed into it. I ignored it and inhaled deeply. This was going to hurt. I pressed my hand firmly against the side of my rib cage where I knew the bones were broken.

The first surge of magick I sent through my hand snapped the rib into place, causing me to cry out at the intense and harsh pain. I panted as my magick continued its painful burning healing as it mended the break back together. I suffered through it, sweat beading on my forehead as I bit my bottom lip hard to keep from whimpering.

The moment it faded away, I clenched my teeth, setting my jaw as I sent another surge down my arm and through my hand. Another rib snapped back into place and I gave another cry, unable to hold it in. My head felt fuzzy and I was faintly aware of a faint booming as Ren tried to break the door down. The burning was intense and I didn't wait for it to calm down before I sent another surge of magick to the broken bones. I held the surge at its peak, forcing more through my hand and the rest of the broken ribs snapped into place.

I nearly blacked out at the pain, a scream dying in my throat as my vision tunnelled rapidly. I felt like I couldn't breathe through the sharp and biting pain that drug through my veins like barbed wire. The burning was just as bad and I found myself curling up into the fetal position, my hands flexing as I buried my face into the pillow as tears blurred my vision. It took a while before the intense burning to stop and when it did I was left panting heavily, my skin sticky with sweat.

I could feel my magick simmer in my veins before it slowly rolled through me, following the path of the pain in soft and warm waves. Its entire focus to soothe me, comfort me as it continued its healing. I relaxed into my bed, my face only twitching with pain as my magick healed the gashes the were had caused with his claws. My breathing slowed, no longer coming in pants and I became aware of Ren's continued growling as he thumped against the door several more times.

I gave a slow stretch, loving the languid and relaxed feeling I had in my muscles and bones as well as the ache in my core at the thought of what would be happening once I opened the door. I had promised Ren that I would be demanding his cock immediately when I was well enough. I slowly moved to sit on my knees. I shook my head, sending my curls cascading around me before I waved my hand at the bedroom door.

It was shoved inwards and Ren stalked his way inside, his muscles tensed as his eyes gleaming with wildness as he looked at me, his chest heaving.

I tilted my head, smiling at him. "You said I wasn't allowed to leave the bed while under your watch." I slowly looked down his form, my eyes resting on his groin and the not so subtle bulge that rested there, I couldn't help how I lightly licked my lips. "I can think of a few activities we could do to keep ourselves...*occupied.*" I flicked my gaze back up to his and he reached out, slamming the bedroom door with a flick of his wrist before he stalked towards me.

I felt a flood of arousal surge through me as I slowly crawled to the edge of the bed, reaching out and grabbing the waist band of his jeans. I looked up at him as I slowly pushed his shirt up, brushing my lips across the lines of his muscles. I pushed it up further and he said nothing as he pulled it off entirely. I nipped at one of the hard lines of muscle next to his hip, soothing the mark with my tongue. I shivered at the taste of him and nuzzled his skin, inhaling his scent deep into my lungs.

I felt a little greedy as I once again grabbed the waist band of his jeans. I undid the button and pulled down the zipper. I wiggled in excitement about the lovely prize waiting for me inside and when I reached for it, Ren grabbed my hands, stopping me.

I looked up at him, tugging against his grip. "Let go." I tried to keep my tone forceful but I couldn't help the edge of pleading my voice had taken. I didn't want to be denied that.

Ren ignored me, wrapping his other arm around my waist as he lifted me up, setting me on my back without a word. I wiggled, agitated with him holding me down and denying me the feeling of his cock on my tongue. "Demanding females do not get what they want." His voice was nearly a low purr and it sent tingles down my body and I became highly aware of just how naked I was.

His lips pressed to my collarbone and I inhaled sharply before trying to kick him in an attempt to get him to release me. "Fuck you, you piece of shit!" I narrowed my eyes feeling a strange urge to hiss at him to express my displeasure. Either that or seriously hurt him. "Let me go!" I struggled against his grip but there was no give and I was not happy with it. My magick sparked amber on my skin and I narrowed my eyes at the were as he trailing his lips down my chest, his grip tightening slightly on my wrists as he did so.

"Smell sweet." He spoke against my skin before he brushed his cheek across the top of my breast, his eyes closed as he huffed as if in bliss.

"Let me go!" I kneed him in the side and he simply grabbed my leg with his other hand, guiding it to wrap around his waist as he ground himself between my legs and heat flared through me like an inferno. I whimpered, unsure of the harshness of of the fabric against the folds of my sex but craving the intensity of the pleasure it brought.

"Bad female." He nipped at my skin, making my breath hitch in my chest as I once again saw those sharply pointed canines in his mouth. "Tease me." He nuzzled my breast before giving it a rather hard bite that I yelped at, the pain searing for a moment before he sucked the skin into his mouth to soothe it with his hot and wicked tongue.

He slowly let it go before he looked up at me, brushing his lips over my throbbing nipple. "Test my patience." His voice became rougher and I arched my back, pushing my breasts closer to him but he simply moved away, leaving me to whimper at the throbbing peaks.

"You better not be doing what I think you are doing." I would not take being tormented like that in bed. I did not play well when it came to orgasm denial and I would fucking bust his balls, literally, if he tried that.

A heavy chuckled rumbled out of him and my runes spun amber as they followed him down, spitting little sparks at him in my anger. "Female is mad... doesn't like being teased." He brushed his nose along the underside of my other breast, I could feel his hot breath on my skin and I could feel my breathing start to deepen in response.

"Fuck you." I spat the words at him even as my chest flushed with my arousal. He was such a fucking prick. I yanked against his grip and barred my teeth.

"Would like that, wouldn't you?" His eyes flicked up to meet mine and I narrowed mine in response. He was just asking to get his ass beat. I paused slightly. Why the hell was I trying to escape him using strength? I internally grinned before I relaxed and let my magick roll through me, focusing it on his hand and within a moment, his hand was forced away from my wrists and I launched at him, shoving him onto his back.

I straddled his chest before kissing him, burying my hands in his hair and holding him close as I sought his tongue out with my own. A deep and rumbling chuckle vibrated his chest as he hands fell to my ass and he kneaded the flesh with strong fingers. He twined his tongue with mine and I groaned into his mouth, loving the feel of him underneath me, loving the feel of his hands on my flesh, stroking and teasing me.

He sat up, holding my ass in his hands as I wrapped my legs around his waist before I grabbed his jaw, nipping at his bottom lip. "Needy." It was an amused word and I didn't even care he was mildly insulting me as I pulled his face towards mine for another mind scrambling kiss.

One of his hands left my ass and I wrapped my arms around him before I gasped as he lifted me up a bit more. His tongue shot forward, chasing mine and I let out a hungry moan as I felt his cock head pressed against my sex, his hand returning to my ass.

He pulled away from me, his eyes meeting mine before he grabbed the back of my neck tightly. "Look at me." It was a harshly said demand and I held his gaze as he slowly lowered me onto his hot and throbbing length. It was hard to maintain eye contact as the pleasure soared through me, that empty feeling in my core being satisfied completely and totally. I was practically writhing, unable to control my own body as he finally settled completely inside me, hilting deep. I could feel him twitching inside of me, could feel his *heartbeat.*

I stared into his eyes, searching for something in his gaze that denied how fucking right it felt for him to be buried inside of me. I wanted to see what everyone else did when they looked at weres. I wanted to see what they felt was so wrong about them because in that moment, with all the feelings that rolled over me, all I could see was a male I would *kill* to spend the rest of my life with.

I didn't understand it, didn't understand why I had thought with him. "What are you doing to me?" The words came out nearly breathless and he buried his face into my neck before he nipped at my earlobe.

His other hand once against grasped a healthy handful of my ass. "Fucking you, witchling." He drew me upwards, his cock sliding against my aching inner walls before he forced me down. I gasped, a cry catching in my throat as he repeated the action. I couldn't help but writhe on him, swirling my hips causing him to grunt and grope my ass as he thrust up into me as I slid back down.

I let my head fall back as I moaned, wrapping my arms around his neck as I arched my back. Ren bent down, drawing one of my nipples into his mouth, suckling hard, his tongue rasping against the tip in the most delicious way. I rode him, matching him thrust for thrust as tension coiled inside me. It was hot and sinful and I didn't ever want it to end but craved the peak it would bring me.

He let my breast go, his hands flexing on my ass before he kissed me. His lips hungry and demanding on my own. I kissed him back, unable to do anything but submit underneath his dominating force. His movements became harsher and mine became more frantic as I chased the peak he was teasing me with. I snapped my hips, rolling them back and forth adding to the sensation before everything tightened to a tiny point and time seemed to stand still before it snapped.

Pleasure rocked my entire body as I let out a cry as the orgasm rocked me. Ren bite down on my neck, feeling the vibrations my throat made as my sex milked his cock, demanding seed from him. He held me down firm in his lap, not letting me move as I clawed at his shoulders and neck, unable to stop myself from raking my nails across his skin as the pleasure seared my body and the inside of my skull to the point of being nearly painful.

I slumped against his chest, my heart beating frantically as I inhaled the air hungrily. He slowly kneaded the flesh of my ass before he slowly laid me down on my back, still tucked firmly inside of me. I let my legs fall from around his waist. I felt tired and completely satisfied but that didn't stop me from whining in displeasure as he pulled out.

I shuddered at the feeling before looking at him. He had an intense look in his eyes as he looked me over. "I'm not done with you yet, female." He grabbed my hips and slowly but firmly turned me over, positioning me on all fours. He wrapped a hand in my hair and pressed himself against me before hilting himself deep with one smooth movement of his hips. I choked off a scream as his pelvis met my ass with a faint smack of flesh on flesh. He pulled back my head with my hair, leaning over me as his other hand grabbed my hip. "Not by a long shot." I gave a groan but arched my back all the same as he started to pull out.

How I would *enjoy* what he would do to me.

Chapter Fifteen
The After Moments

I shifted on the bed behind BamBam, feeling completely relaxed after our intense session of sex. I took a fair amount of pride in the fact I had gotten the mouthy witch to beg me over and over again. I trailed my hand down her side, enjoying the feeling of her skin underneath my palm.

I didn't usually linger after breeding. We would finish and I would leave, unable to stay due to my position as Bo's protector. I never stayed in the bed with the female, never basked in the feeling sex always gave me. I was finding it rather... enjoyable.

"Thinking about anything in particular?" Her voice was husky and almost raspy and I fought back a satisfied grin at the sound of it. I knew it sounded like that from her repeated screams and cries and begging I had forced upon her as I fucked her. I knew she had enjoyed every second of my domination and that made the satisfaction so much headier.

I brushed my nose along the back of her neck, enjoying the sweat and sex scent that coated her usually sweet scent. "No."

"Basking are you?" At her cheeky question I merely grunted, digging my fingers into her side. My eyes going hooded at the feeling of her skin in my grip. Her flesh was so pliable and soft, much different than the last female I had. Faes were always willowy and their skin tight over their slightly muscular form. They were enjoyable but my fingers never really sunk into their flesh like they did with BamBam. "Are you up for another round?" There was an edge of expectation to her voice and I slid my hand around her waist, palming one of her breasts.

"Are you?" I lazily squeezed it, enjoying her slight whimper as I deliberately scrapped my rough hand against her sensitive nipple as it pebbled and nearly throbbed. I had teased those peaks until she begged me to stop so I could only imagine how much they pained her.

She grabbed my hand and slowly removed it from her breast as she let out a small huff. "You make a compelling argument and I will concede this point for now." I captured her hand in mine, lifting it up, extending her arm. I nuzzled her shoulder, looking at the runes that pulsed a faint yellow on her skin.

"Why do they have colours?" I rubbed her dainty hand with my fingers before I grasped her wrist, stroking one of the runes with my thumb, it fluttered a faint pink underneath my touch.

She made a small hum in her throat as she turned her head, moving her hand as the runes danced along her skin and over her palm. "I'm not sure." She rolled her head, her eyes catching mine. "They have always been like that." Her cheeks pinkened slightly as if she were embarrassed. "It's a bit difficult to deal with because it makes nearly impossible to lie." Her green eyes shimmered as she looked at me.

"Good to know." I captured her lips with mine, cupping her face with my hand as I leaned over her. I liked the thought the female couldn't easily lie to me. I didn't like dealing with deceptive females. It always got messy. She made an appreciative sound in her throat, her hand running through my hair and her nails scratching at my scalp. I shivered at the feeling before pulling back from the kiss.

She made a small humming sound. "A girl could get addicted to that." Her voice was breathless as her eyes fluttered open and a faint flush touched her cheeks and neck. I shifted so I was lying on my back, my arm behind my head as I stared at the ceiling. She moved as well, rolling over and snuggling up against me, her head on my chest.

I wrapped my arm around her back, rubbing against her soft skin. I wanted to run my face across the silk like skin she held, marking it with my scent to warn other males to back off. She trailed her fingers across my chest, tracing my muscles lightly. A rather comfortable silence fell and I wondered if this was how males with females usually felt. My instinct was quiet on the subject. It would urge me to continue to feast and breed the female but it knew that she wasn't compatible with us and we would leave when that slightly bitter scent got too much to handle.

The silence brought to mind all that she had said in her stupor the night before. I narrowed my eyes at the remembrance. "You said there was no cure for what the End Bringer did." We had all been told about Rowenya and how she was the one to bring such destruction to us as a species. The End Bringer, the doom of our species.

She paused, her hand stilling in its small motions before she nodded. "I did." She continued her tracing and I let out an irritated rumble that she gave a slight chuckle at. She nipped my pectoral, drawing her tongue across one of my scars and I felt a coiling in my gut as my cock responded to the heated action.

I reached down and pinched her chin in my fingers before making her look at me. "Explain." A growl rumbled my chest at her rather petulant look before she rolled her eyes and huffed.

"*Fine.*" It was said in such an exasperated tone that I itched to smack her ass for it but she shifted beside me sitting up before straddling my stomach. Her tousled curls bounced around her, her form bare to my gaze as she looked down at me. "Rowenya was born an only child to elderly parents." She made a slight face and I grasped her hips, stroking her skin with my thumbs. I liked the position she had taken. Heat flared through me, creating a heaviness in my groin. "They died when she was young and she was taken into a Coven at a very young age. It was said she used to sneak out to the Forests when she grew older, feeling confined behind the stone walls." She settled slightly, her expression softening.

"I know how that feels. Being trapped in a place that doesn't understand who you are. It's grating." There was a faint not of sombre reflection before she shrugged it off. "Anyway on her little travels she met a weremale by the name of Ragnor."

"End Keeper." I inclined my head slightly. He had been a powerful male in his time, the High King of High Kings. Many had coveted his position and he was betrayed because of it.

"Why do you call him that?" She tilted her head as she looked down at me, her gaze shining with curiosity.

"He was the thing that stood between the End Bringer and our doom." He had been all that stood between her and our end and he had been removed. "He was taken and she was left to decimate our species." A curse that killed our females as they grew within the womb, a terrible curse that destroyed our species by denying us females we highly coveted.

Her eyebrows pinched together. "Not taken." She shook her head, pinching her lips together as she looked down at me, "Ragnor left her."

I shook my head firmly at the insinuation. "No." I was confused as to why she would claim he would leave her. Ragnor had been the best of our species, the most proud. He would never have left his female while rounded with his babe.

"Yes, that's why she was all upset and went all doom bringer before she was burned." She looked at me as if I were simple and I shook my head again.

"He filled her with his seed, it took within her. The only thing that would stop a weremale from returning to his breeder after that is death or capture." I palmed her lower stomach, imagining my babe taking in there and knowing there would be nothing in this world that would ever stop me from being by her side as she created new life. "The End Keeper was taken from her." Taken from her and forced to endure the greatest punishment of all. The feeling of failing his breeder and offspring as both were murdered while he was trapped and helpless.

"By who?" Her voice lowered and I squeezed her hips, liking how interested she was in were history. It wasn't often anyone was.

I shrugged. "One of the High Kings who coveted his place." A male who thought he was more than he was and he doomed our entire species. "We don't know the original betrayer and it has been lost to time but it is said the End Keeper was locked away in a forgotten castle, chained up and forced to endure his beloved's death." The thought raked against my instinct like it had been drug over red hot coals. To be forced to endure ultimate punishment was unheard of and malicious. The betrayer's line was lucky we did not know who they were because they would have been wiped out for their treachery.

"That's... fucking sad." Her bottom lip stuck out slightly, her expression tinged with what looked to be empathy as she looked down at me, her runes flickered a rather alarming black as they sunk down her body, falling from their previous high spots.

I squeezed her hips once more, shifting beneath her to distract her from her sombre thoughts. "Why have you been taught different?" It was strange that she would have been taught such a strange illusion of what happened. Rowenya had been a treasure of our species, our forefathers had laid down their swords at her feet and she had been called the Uniter before the curse had befallen us by her hands.

"I dunno." She gave a lazy shrug before giving a flippant gesture. "Probably some warlocks all jealous that you guys know how to fuck better than them and wanted to scare witches off of your species by claiming you aren't monogamous." Her mouth turned up in a cheeky grin and I felt a chuckle rumble my chest before I leaned up, kissing her hungrily. I liked it when she praised me above her pathetic warlocks.

I pulled back before chuckling. "You are scared by the thought of... polygamy?" It was amusing at best, such a strong species to be scared of *sharing*.

She lifted her chin, gazing down her nose at me. "Witches are notoriously monogamous." Her tone was haughty and just a bit snotty and it reminded me much of the witches I had known before but her eyes sparkled at me with mirth.

"Warlocks have harems." I tilted my head, narrowing my eyes slightly as I watched as all the mirth and amusement disappeared from her gaze.

"A *stupid* practice and if any witch finds herself in one she would be aware that she might get exploded by an irate wife." Th words were spat out with a rather large amount of derision and hate.

I raised an eyebrow at her sudden passion. "And the warlock? Does he not receive punishment?" I smirked slightly as she gave a firm nod.

"He should be lucky to find himself dead because if not he would have his bits and pieces removed and hung up on his wife's mantle, above her throne, before the rest of him would be slathered in honey and shoved in a barrel with fire ants and maggots as he is forcibly fed milk." At the rather archaic punishment I found my lips curling up. Such a *feisty* female.

"Suitable." I found it to be a perfectly suitable punishment. Any male who willingly walked out on his breeder for another was the lowest of the species, were or not.

She dissolved into giggles as eyes twinkled with pleasure and her runes flashed pink. She bent down, tucking her hair behind her ear before giving me a slow and lingering kiss that had a rumble growing in my chest as I dug my nails into her skin, holding her close. She pulled back, licking her lips with a hum of enjoyment before she heaved out a breath. "But back to the original topic. There is no cure because Rowenya was the last of her bloodline and Bo is a were. You need either the blood or the soul to remove the curse." She gave a firm nod and I shook my head.

"There is a magic soul within her." I knew it was there, she had abilities that no other were had. I could sens the magick within her.

"Maybe a part of it but not enough." She gave a slow shrug, her breasts moving in a rather tantalizing fashion as I realized they were bare and waiting for a hot mouth to lavish them with attention. "A full soul would be in a witch, not a werewolf. My best guess is they are pandering to false hope in the off chance their 'cure' might work but it won't." She gave me a broad grin. "My second guess is that only males were involved in the decision making process because any standard witch would tell them it's bullshit." I quirked my eyebrow at her, showing my skepticism and she dissolved into giggled once more, leaning over and burying her face in my neck as the giggles turned into laughter.

She pulled away, the green of her eyes nearly dancing with her cheerful mood as her runes danced yellow on her skin. "You're right. You're right." She wiped at her eyes, faint giggles escaping her as she did so. "No witch besides me would have the balls to tell them it is a stupid idea." She smiled brightly at that and I sat up with a nod. I didn't doubt she would be the only female willing to tell a group of weres and warlocks that they were fucking stupid.

I kissed her slowly, more than ready and willing for another round. Her arms locked around my neck as she twirled her tongue around mine, lapping at it as she wiggled in my lap, signalling her own readiness for another bout of sex. I slid my hands down to cup her generous ass. How I loved those curves, their fullness and give. I also loved the view it gave me when I looked down to see my cock sliding into her before my pelvis his her ass to ripple her flesh as she gave a throaty moan.

"Bam?" Bo's voice had BamBam pulling away, her expression suddenly glowing as she looked over her shoulder to the little intruder.

"Hey, baby!" Her tone was crooning and soft as she shifted off of me, her entire attention on the little female. "You want to grab me my robe so we can cuddle?" At the words Bo's expression practically beamed before she bolted back into the main room in search of the roe that BamBam had hung up in the bathroom.

I couldn't help how my lip curled up at the throbbing of my cock. It was painful and I knew I would have no recourse for it as BamBam gave me a quick peck on the lips before shoving me towards the edge of the bed. "Out, Ren. It's girl time!" She bounced out of bed and I was left groaning at the sight it inspired before my jeans were thrown at my head as she pulled on some underwear, covering herself from view. I huffed and moved out of the bed, putting on the pants with a faint growl.

"Gots it!" Bo burst into the room, the robe clutched tightly in her little hands as she held it out for

BamBam. The witchling took it, kissing her forehead before waving her hand at the bed. The magick sparked in the air as it ran over the bed, cleaning away our activities and turning down the bed with the scent of clean linens. "Get into bed and we will cuddle." Bo giggled as she jumped onto the large bed, grinning at me with her white little teeth.

I walked around the bed, chucking her underneath the chin before I found myself moving towards BamBam as she pulled her robe on. I slid an arm around her waist, nuzzling her neck. "We will finish later." I ground myself slightly against her ass as I drew my teeth across her neck.

She turned her head, kissing me softly before a teasing smirk tugged up her mouth. "And I look forward to it." She patted my ass as she moved to the bed, sitting down on it before opening her arms for the little female to crawl into. I walked away but unable to stop myself from watching how my little female snuggled right up close to the witch with all the trust in the world and how the witch's runes rapidly pulsated a pleased pink as she trailed patterns across my little female's exposed skin. I felt my mouth turn up at the sight.

The witch was right. She couldn't lie, not to me.

Chapter Sixteen
Stuck Up Witches

I watched as Bo ran around outside of the cabin. She was enjoying the open meadow, running around in the wildflowers, her yellow dress snapping behind her as she would roll and tumble while laughing happily. It made me smile to see her so joyful. I could only imagine the hell she had lived while being hunted down by the witches and werewolves. Never given a chance to be a child or to be happy, always wary and on the run. That was no life for a child.

My gaze flicked to where Ren paced in the shadows of the trees. He had been doing that since he had gotten out of bed. It was as if he was trying to figure out just where I had taken us. It was further north, farther away from the settlements. I had remembered it from one of my family trips my mother had taken us on. It had been just enough of a memory to jump everything through the portal.

I knew that if we stayed for too long then someone might find us but I also knew that it would take them weeks to get a location due to the ley lines I sat the cabin on. The natural magick of the earth would confuse any and all locator spells that would be used. Not enough to hide us forever but enough to give us some time. With how close Florence and her were puppet had been, Bo and Ren had needed the time.

I made a slight face at the reminder of the stuck up bitch. If there was any witch I was glad to kill, it was that trumped up excuse of a level six witch. She walked around with her nose in the air as if she were the greatest shit since magick began. Her attitude was shit and I was glad I was able to wipe that stupid smug look off her face.

My gaze found Bo once more as she did a cartwheel, giggling happily. I found a smile on my face as I looked at her. "Hey, Bo-peep." At my words her gaze snapped to me and she beamed before skipping towards me. She grabbed my hands once she was close enough, grinning up at me. "Do you want to bake some cookies?" At the question her face lit up and she nodded enthusiastically.

"Honey bunches of hotness." I called the words out and Ren stopped pacing, turning immediately and stalking towards me, that stern look on his face that spoke of his agitation.

The silly male didn't quite like not knowing exactly where we were. I enjoyed his irritation immensely, I found it to be payback for his repeated orgasm denial that he knew I hated. His expression didn't change as he came over, hovering over me as he wrapped an arm around my waist and pulling me close. He nuzzled his nose against my neck and I tilted my head, allowing him more access. "I'm going to go shopping."

His chest rumbled and he drug his teeth across my skin in warning. "No." He said it rather petulantly and I fought back a smirk.

"I will be right back." I winced slightly as he pinched the skin of my neck with his teeth.

Bo let my hands go before pushing at Ren. "No, Bapa! Gunna make cookies." She bared her teeth at him and Ren let my neck go, looking down at the small female.

"*No.*" That petulant tone was once back in his voice and my mouth twitched upwards.

"It's gunna happen, Ren." I pushed away from him but his arm tightened around my waist. I looked up at him. "I'm not a witch you say no to." My magick snapped against his chest as I shoved at it and he jumped back, his eyes narrowing at me.

I ignored him as I bent down and cupped Bo's face, kissing her cheeks, making exaggerated kissing sounds as I did so. "I'll be right back, beauty." Without waiting for them to speak I waved my hand, a portal opening up as my magick surged through me and I stepped through it.

The supermarket was brightly lit and the portal closed behind me as I moved down the aisle. I waved my hand and a small portal opened up to my kitchen. I grabbed various things off of the shelf, throwing them through the portal. It followed me as I moved around the store. I didn't particularly care about the humans that were giving me strange looks as I grabbed a bag of flour and put it through the portal before doing the same with a large bag of sugar.

I made sure to get everything we needed to make cookies before doing another round of the store, grabbing the staples we needed for the cabin. I made eye contact with one the male clerks as I tossed a flat of soup through the portal and I knew the little human wanted to say something about it. I smirked, giving the male a wink as I sauntered off towards the breakfast aisle. A ripple of unease washed down my back and my magick paused, sensing a disturbance in the air. I immediately closed down the portal, I knew what the fuck that meant.

Four level six witches appeared, lunging for where the portal had been and giving equally loud shouts of frustration when they were too late. They whirled on me and I crossed my arms over my chest, smirking at the furious witches. I loved fucking with them and I didn't want them on my home turf.

"You open that portal right back up!" The witch to the left spat the words at me and I blinked at her as innocently as I could.

"Portal to where? I don't remember there being a portal." I gave a slow shrug, looking around just as slow as if utterly confused by her words.

Another witch grabbed my arm, spinning me back around, her finger shoved in my face. "You can't play stupid, Miranda!" I grimaced at her bright orange nail and slapped her hand away from my face.

"You are right, you do that well enough for us both, June." I gave the witch a wide grin and her expression darkened with anger.

"You little bitch!" She lifted her hand one one of the other witches grabbed her arm, hissing at her to calm down. I smirked as she yanked her arm away from the other witch, glowering at me intensely.

The witch who stopped June looked at me as she pushed to the front of the group. I knew all their names, I just didn't particularly care to remember at the moment. "You do know that what you are doing is treasonous, right?" Her words were low and I tilted my head as I looked at her. I found it amusing they were all wearing standard witches robes. I fought back a laugh, they looked stupid.

"You know me, if it's not treasonous it's not worth my time!" I gave her a broad grin and I could see her jaw tick with agitation.

"Have you no shame in your actions?" She hissed the words at me and I shook my head.

"Absolutely none." I glanced around to the others and their agitated expressions. "Because the look on your stupid faces makes it worth it."

"You are fuc-" She stopped herself, swallowing hard as her face twisted with disgust. "You are *fraternizing* with a werewolf." She said the words like I should care but I honestly didn't give two shits what they thought. "That's a burnable offence." She emphasized the word and I shrugged.

"I know. Florence let me know that." I felt a satisfied grin cross my face as I looked at the witch. "Before I splattered her." All over my walls, that stupid snooty bitch was gone for good and I was fucking happy about that.

She sputtered. "You did *what?*" I could see her face grow more red as she looked at me. "She was a member of the council! You can't just-!"

"I'm *banished.*" I emphasized the word before I smiled at her. "I can do whatever the hell I want."

"You are lucky we don't cart you off to Coven Thirteen for your behaviour!" June's voice shook with rage and I turned, looking her up and down.

"Wanting to give Elder Irma a new toy to play with?" I narrowed my eyes at her, Coven Thirteen was where they sent those they didn't want to hear from again. Elder Irma was a rank old bitch.

"You are fucking a werewolf!" One of the previously quiet witches shouted it out, her face red with rage as she shook, her hands clenched into fists.

"You should try it some time. Might cause some of you stuck up bitches to loosen up." I enjoyed the horrified looks they got on their faces as I said it. I wasn't entirely sure why they were acting so prudishly, I knew pretty much all witches opened up their legs for one male or another. Being a 'pure' female wasn't a requirement to be an Elder. If it was, more than ninety percent of them would lose their positions.

"I think we need to test for her contraceptive spell." June's tone was spiteful as she looked at me, her eyes narrowed to slits. "Make sure she isn't making half-breed abominations." At the venomous words I lunged, slamming my fist into her face and enjoying the sound of her nose snapping. I wouldn't have her deriding any of my children like that, existing or not. No one talked shit about me or my own.

I watched as the rest of them tried to help June as she staggered, blubbering about her nose as it leaked blood. "If any of you bitches touch me I will fucking kill you all." My magick crackled on the surface of my skin rather aggressively. "My babies will be adorable! Regardless of their father and I won't let you defile them before they are even born!" There was no way in *hell* I would allow any stuck up witch spit shit about my children before they are even born.

"My, my... things are getting a little heated." At the smooth and refined voice I whirled around but was suddenly stopped, my entire focus on a set of mesmer crystals that floated in the air in front of my face. I swallowed, staring at their glimmering surface, unable to think or move as they swirled in the air and darkness coated my vision suddenly and I knew nothing more.

I shot upright in a bed with with a curse in my mouth. "Motherfucker!" I had been straight up fucking kidnapped.

Me!

I had no clue how the fuck that could happen. I wasn't the stupid bimbo type that fell for mesmer crystals so it really pissed me off. My magick sparked down my skin, following the amber runes as they moved rapidly. I looked around and hesitated. I was in a rather luxurious and opulent bedroom. Silk curtains hung on the canopy bed and I was fairly positive I was laying on satin sheets.

I blinked, confusion overtaking my anger as I took in my surroundings. I moved to get off the bed when the feeling of the sheets moving against my skin made me pause. I shouldn't have felt the sensation that well. I looked down and my eyes widened in angry disbelief. "*Motherfucker*!" I had been stripped of my clothes and someone had put a light green lingerie set on me. I stumbled out of the bed and looked down again with outrage.

It didn't matter that the bra cupped my breast perfectly and the cheeky panties perfectly showed off my ass. What mattered was some asshole stripped me naked and changed my clothes without my consent. I let out an angry huff, glowering as I looked around, my magick's anger reaching the tipping point.

I grabbed one of the posts of the bed and my magick surged through me, splintering the wood underneath my hand in its rage. I swung out with my other hand and the large mirror above what looked to be a vanity dresser shattered as my magick slammed into it.

I liked the sound of the destruction as I dropped my hand from the splintered canopy bed and shoved my hand towards the vanity dresser itself. I could feel my magick wrap around it and I shot my hand out to the side, sending the large, and probably very expensive, dresser through the double balcony doors. I narrowed my eyes and held out my arms, letting my magick surge through me with my anger and outrage and all the furniture started vibrating before each piece imploded into bits of fabric and splinters of wood.

Once the air cleared of the sounds of splintering wood, smashing glass, and ripping fabric I let my arms drop, feeling much better. I put my hands on my hips and looked around at the destruction I had caused. It made me very happy to see all the lavish decor and furniture ruined beyond repair. It served whichever asshole kidnapped me right for locking me up and taking a look at my goodies without my *express* permission.

"Some of those pieces were centuries old." At the refined and smooth voice I whirled around and a *very* attractive warlock leaned against the doorjamb, looking over the destruction. I took in his lean but muscular form, strong jaw, straight nose, and dark hair that looked like it *begged* to have fingers run through it. He finished his look around the room before his crystal blue eyes landed on me with a small sigh. "But if my queen does not like them and wishes to redecorate, who am I to deny her?" I was so busy looking him over with a bit of stark appreciation that I nearly missed what he said.

"*Excuse me?*" I snapped my gaze back up to his face and blinked rapidly in disbelief. I was fairly positive I did not just hear what I thought I heard.

"I said who am I to deny you." He waved his hand and a glass of red wine floated into the open doorway before he grasped it, taking a sip as he looked me over. I was never one to deny a male a look but I was so caught off-guard by him and his words that I felt a bit over exposed. No matter how attractive he was, he knew exactly what he said and he was playing games.

I crossed my arms over my chest, lifting my chin and narrowing my eyes. My moment of being caught off-guard was gone. "You don't want me to repeat myself." I dared him to ignore me a second time.

"Redecorating." He raised a dark eyebrow at me before taking another sip of wine and pushing off the door jam, the movements fluid and graceful. He gestured to the ruined room with his cup. "As my queen you will live here and if you are unhappy with the accommodations you are well within your right to reduce the room to rubble." He gave an unconcerned shrug and took another drink of wine as he looked at me, his eyes going hooded as he looked me over once more.

"Who the hell are you to take liberties with *my* titles?" My magick once again crackled to life underneath my anger. "I *am* a motherfucking queen but who the hell are you to say I am *your* queen?" Miranda never played that way and BamB'am certainly fucking wouldn't. I set my jaw as I narrowed my eyes at him further.

He inclined his head at me. "I apologize, I am getting ahead of myself." He let go of the wine glass and it floated in the air as he gave a courtly bow in my direction. "My name is Mercutio Anadori, level Seven Elder Warlock and King of the Covens. At your service, my lady." He stood up from the bow and I looked him over once more, raising my eyebrow at his attire. Should have guessed the suave bastard was royalty. He practically oozed arrogance and finery.

"Do you give all females you kidnap that lip service or am I special?" I couldn't keep the snark out of my tone and his moth lifted into a rather sexy smirk that I had to internally slap myself for appreciating.

"Oh, Miranda, you are *very* special." The name made all slightly warming feelings disappear and I immediately stiffened.

"BamBam." The name came out clipped and I glowered at him darkly. A better smooth talking asshole would have known that little tidbit of information before even approaching me.

"I beg your pardon?" It was his turn to look taken aback and I fought down a smirk at the look on his face.

"My name is BamBam." I huffed slightly. I had been BamBam for *years* and the fact people still called me Miranda was irksome. It was also one way to get into my poor graces.

"Ahhhh, apologies." He made a fist over his heart before giving me another bow. I rolled my eyes at it but made sure to clear my expression as he straightened, grasping his wine glass from where it floated. "You are a very special witch, BamBam." He waved his hand and a path from him to me cleared of debris and I felt my lip curling up into a sneer as he started to walk towards me.

"I know. What's your point?" I stared at him hard. The asshole kidnapped me, changed my fucking clothes, and presumed to tell me I was his queen. I wanted to make a face at that.

I had a perfectly good life where I was.. well I had to admit it wasn't perfect. I had been lonely, stuck with a shitty ass truck that continually wanted to die on me, and had no gold. Not to mention that I hadn't been allowed to go to my usual places or see my family. Banishment sucked but that didn't mean I wanted some douche-y royal claiming me as if I would precipitate the change in luxury.

He reached my side, grasping my chin in his hand gently and I jerked away from his touch, glowering at him darkly. "Fiery witch." He let out a small chuckle. "My point is that sometimes certain witches get overlooked because they might not follow the rules to the letter. You are a strong witch, BamBam, and I doubt you have been fully appreciated." I couldn't argue with that, people rarely appreciated talent. He waved his free hand, clearing the floor of debris before pressing his hand to my lower back.

I nearly jumped at the contact before smoothly moving away. "No touching." I was currently on a werewolf only sex diet and I didn't say he could touch me.

He inclined his head towards me. "Apologies, BamBam. Let us go to the balcony." He gestured with his hand and I stared at him, trying to figure out what his angle was but he seemed simply content and at ease and I slowly moved towards the busted double doors. I smirked at that, I hoped it hurt him to see that destruction. The cool air moved over my skin and I shivered slightly. "I am sorry. I was so enthralled by your beauty I forgot you might get cold being so exposed." He placed his jacket over my shoulders and I settled into the jacket. I wasn't about to argue with him because I was nearly nude and I didn't like being cold.

He waved his hand once more and the balcony was cleared of debris. It was clear he had a substantial amount of power but I could also see it was more than likely due to the fact he had a signet ring. A magickally crafted item that acted as a tuner for his magick and allowed him to work it without the normal tools.

"So, are you going to continue telling me why I am here or will I have to shove you over the railing?" I was feeling the itch to do just that and he merely chuckled, looking at me as he smiled.

"No need for that, BamBam." He leaned against the railing, setting his wine glass down. "I am in need of a queen and only the most powerful witch will do. We have seven levels of magick but I know that if we had more, you would still be at the top." I didn't particularly believe that he kidnapped me to issue a marriage proposal. I had been in the Covens for a long time before I was banished so I knew he wanted something and I had a feeling it had to do with the two werewolves who were currently in my cabin.

"If you were my queen you would rule over all the Territories." He gave a sweeping gesture to the view before us and I actually turned to look at it. We were high up in a castle tower, the land rolled out from the stone walls that encased the Warlock King's Castle and the view was so spectacular it nearly took my breath away. "You would have legions of servants at your beck and call to do everything in their power to make sure you are happy and satisfied in your life." That did sound pretty fucking awesome but still, he wanted something from me and I didn't like how he was dancing around the issue.

I turned away from the glorious view to look at him as I gave a sweet smile. "You would offer the position of Witch Queen to a banished witch who has been regularly fucked by a werewolf?" I deliberately kept my words crass just to watch how he would react but he merely waved his hand as if waving my words off.

"You are young and a rebel. You had the ability to remove your contraceptive charm but you didn't. As far as I am concerned, you have merely been exploring your sexuality with the limited options available to you." He looked at me, his mouth quirking up as well as his eyebrow as if to say, the ball is in your court.

I narrowed my eyes at his slight challenge. "Think you can exceed his performance?" It would be a damn near impossible performance to match, let alone exceed. "Or am I to have a litany *of* servants to cater to me while you service your harem?" I gave him another smile but was unable to help how brittle it turned as I looked at him. I knew how warlocks were and I wouldn't be second place to my husband. I would require total fidelity and the only male who ever even hinted at that was Ren, a fucking werewolf. The warlock was so out of his element it wasn't even funny.

He picked up his glass once more, turning to look at me completely, his hip resting against the railing. "You are more witch than a hundred harems. I would have my hands quite full with you as my wife." He winked at me as he took a drink of his wine before sliding closer to me, brushing a lock of my hair behind my ear. I shivered at the slight contact. "Besides, you have offered me a challenge and I refuse to be outshone by a *werewolf*. I am king, I need to excel in *all* aspects of my life." The words were low and heated as he bent down and spoke them by my ear.

I sniffed and turned away from him to look at the view again. "I've had warlock. Not too keen." I had quite a few and I knew how they played out. I knew their entire playbook and there was *no* shifting in tactics with them.

He slid an arm around my waist and pulled me close. "You haven't had me." At the low and rasping words I gave another sniff and he replied with a low chuckle that brushed over my ear. "Do you think that werewolf will stay with you? He will pack up and leave when he grows bored of you and he will. You aren't compatible with him and his instinct will drive him to find a female he can have offspring with. That means leaving *you.*" His grip grew a bit tighter and I frowned. I understood what he was saying and I knew it was true. It had been that nagging little thought in the back of my head that warned me to not get attached.

"If you give him and the carrier up, you can live by my side as my queen and I would pamper you endlessly and lavish you with all the affection, attention, and passion you could desire." His voice was low and compelling and I stared at the rolling green hills that were slowly being hidden by an embankment of fog. "You could give me a line of sons. Our species *needs* this cure. Imagine having a bouncing little boy in your arms before the year is out, an *heir* to this throne." I could imagine a little boy, one that smiled and giggled as I chased him through the meadows.

"You give me a chance at that with you and I will give you anything you desire." His lips brushed the shell of my ear and I gave a small start at his words. Anything I desired was a hefty price he was willing to pay for my cooperation.

I turned to look at him, a slow smile crossing my face. "Anything?"

His blue eyes were heated with desire and intensity as he leaned closer. "*Anything.*" I found my smile deepening.

Perfect.

Chapter Seventeen
The Witching Moon

I paced back and forth, staring at the door. BamBam had been gone for hours. I felt my muscles tense as my instinct crawled through my limbs like my unruly beast. The longer the witchling was gone the more risk there was to Bo and I. I didn't know where we were, I didn't know where we could go. The witchling had taken us far away, somewhere that the air was colder and crisp. I could smell the faint magick in the ground but I couldn't place us.

My eyes darted around the room as I inhaled deeply, trying to get a read on anything that I could. Bo was eating a sandwich, her focus intent on it. I had fed her to keep her quiet. She asked constantly about the witch and I couldn't handle her voice, my ears becoming sensitive as I tried to listen.

Dangerous

My instinct rasped the word against my nerves and I bared my teeth, there was too many things that could go wrong. I narrowed my eyes, my beast rumbling his alertness as he was pulled from his slumber, my instinct succeeding in rousing him. I wondered fro a brief moment if the witchling had been taken. I knew the tactics weres used to make enemies talk, I had used many myself. The thought of her being harmed in such a way to speak made my muscles twitch with agitation.

    I gave in and moved towards the front of the cabin, glancing back at Bo. A flash of a gleam was all it took before a snarl erupted from my chest, my beast shoving forward. "Go!" I boomed the word at Bo and she inhaled sharply and bolted for the back room. I felt my bones and muscles shift and twist in my body before my beast drew back and rammed the front door, the wood splintering as he sought out the beast that presumed to hunt us.

    Lights flashed in the air rapidly and we could see witches and weres in the brief moments of brightness. We were surrounded. My beast shook his head, aiming for the closest body, claws ripping and tearing as the slight female screamed and twisted, trying to escape a death that was already upon her.

    He shifted, feeling the crackle of magic in the air as chanting erupted, shattering the silence of the night. We felt the charge build in the air and I urged my bloodthirsty beast right. He dove into a group of weres right as the lightning struck the earth, colliding with one of the weres we jumped behind.

    Shouting and snarls joined the chanting as more and more bodies fell to our claws. We couldn't let them get close to Bo, we had protect her. My instinct was hissing at us so loudly it was like a buzz behind our eyes. The scent of blood and viscera coated the air thickly and we grinned with bloody teeth as we used the flashing lights to our advantage.

Bo's angry scream shattered through everything and my heart twisted and turned in my chest.

Prrrrooteeeect

My instinct roared it at me and I took control, shifting down from my beast before bolting towards the cabin. Several weres had a hold of her, letting her dangle as she fought and growled, her little teeth sinking into large hands as her eyes flashed yellow with her tiny beast.

Proooooooooteeeeeect

My instinct's roar grew so loud it shook my vision as I sped closer to her, trying to reach her. She turned her head towards me, her eyes widening with terror. "Bapa!" Her little hand outstretched for me right as a silver net was thrown over me. I scented the weapon too late, unable to dodge it and the metal hissed and burned against my flesh, the weight of it sending me to the ground.

Protect

My instinct grew muffled, its words fading in my mind. I struggled to stay upright but the metal sapped my strength and blurred my vision as it seared into my skin, burning deep.

I lifted my head, baring my teeth and letting out a rattling snarl as dark shapes approached. "Shut up." The voice was sneering before a heavy boot connected with my temple and everything went black.

Consciousness came back to me with the feeling of cold water against my skin. My vision blurred and I could scent my own burned flesh as the silver wrapped around me destroyed the flesh it touched. I looked up and my heart stilled in my chest. Bo stood on top of an altar, her little arms outstretched as chains wrapped around her wrists, holding her in place between two dark pillars.

The witching moon hung large and full behind her. "Bo!" Her name was nothing but a rasp and she didn't even flinch, her face was still and expressionless as she looked as though she stared into oblivion.

"Oh she can't hear you." At BamBam's voice I snapped my head to the side and she looked down at me, her head tilted as a smirk rested on her full lips. "I made sure to do the spell myself so it's on there good." I looked down her and realized no wounds marred her and no chains encased her.

Rage erupted in my stomach and seared through my veins at her betrayal. The witchling had betrayed us, betrayed Bo, betrayed *me*. The silver chains dug further into my skin as I struggled, snarling at her. I knew I never should have trusted her, never should have let her close.

Witches were a curse!

I growled heavily, trying to fight through the mind numbing pain to reach the strength to kill her for what she had done.

She seem unfazed by my struggling as she flicked her braid behind her back. "I know. I know. But they offered me a castle and to be queen. I mean, come on." She gave a flippant gesture with her hand. "That's one hell of an offer."

"Vile!" I spat the word out, it was garbled and hard to understand but I wanted the witch to see my depths of hate I had for her.

She simply looked away towards where Bo was standing, her small white dress fluttering slightly in the breeze. I realized why the little bitch looked away when flames erupted from the various scones and seven warlocks dressed in black started towards the altar. Chanting slowly filled the air and the magick crackled against my skin.

"Touch her and die!" I snarled the words out, fighting against he silver chains, struggling to find the strength to escape to save Bo.

My heart thudded in my chest. I had protected her when she was but a tiny infant and they were going to force me into the greatest punishment. I snapped my teeth so hard my vision rattled. My gaze found the weres that stood off to the side. They were more vile than the warlocks that slowly moved towards my little female.

"No honour!" I bellowed the words out but there wasn't even a flinch to their forms. "Ragnor curse you!" I struggled harder.

"You should really thank me." The witch's voice drew my attention back to her and there was a heavy amusement to her tone. I struggled to get to my knees, trying to lunge for her but the silver stopped the movements.

"Moon *curse* you! Die by my teeth!" My vision was nearly red as I stared at the female who betrayed me and my little female.

"You know, as nice as a castle is and how great it would be to be queen, what really sold me on helping them was that they said I could kill you after the ceremony was done." She gave a lazy smirk at that, giving me a wink. I growled heavily managing to get to my knees and using the rage to propel me to my feet. I went to dive at the female but she dove first. Her momentum knocked me down, rolling us both behind the stone steps of the altar. I snarled at her but she seemed unfazed as she covered my ears with her hands and pressed her face to my chest, hunching her shoulders towards her own.

I struggled to throw her off, hating that she was muffling my hearing. I tried to move my head to tear into her wrist when a heavy boom rattled the air and the force shook my bones as fire erupted over where we were, the heat of it was enough to make me flinch away. The witchling removed her hands, looking up as screams filled the air, her face angular and edges as magick gathered around her.

She looked down at me, grabbing at the chains that held me tight. "I fucking *love* the witching moon." Her eyes gleamed and her teeth flashed and my instinct roused slowly, free from the silver.

Be wary

She grinned at me, and the shadows added maniacal edge to her expression as she stood up.

Female is deadly

Chapter Eighteen
Boss Ass Bitch

I headed towards the stairs quickly, my magick building in me with my excitement. I could smell burned flesh and ash that hung in the air. The sounds of screams of pain filled my ears and rolled over me with delight. I looked to where Ren lay on the ground, his beautiful flesh marked by the burns of the silver.

I snapped my hand out, my magick immediately wrapping around him, sinking into his skin to remove those nasty marks and replace the strength that had been sapped from him. I wished they wouldn't have used silver but there was only so much I could get away with.

"Allowing me to kill you after is what sold me on it, honey bunches of hotness, because I knew they were too stupid to realize I would fuck them over." As if I would get rid of my sexy were for some stupid, cocky, and *arrogant* warlock. I knew how to handle my little were toy, my eyes flicked down to his junk and my lip tugged upwards.

Correction, not so little.

There was no way I was going to take a warlock's word on keeping me satisfied when I had a sure fire male to do that already.

I turned away from him dashing up the stairs as my magick surged through me, the witching moon that hung in the air fuelling it just as much as my emotions. I looked towards Bo and her gaze landed on me and she giggled, waving her little hand in the chains, a smile crossing her face.

Satisfaction rolled through me at the pillars of charred ass that surrounded her. I could see the runes I had painstakingly drawn on her slowly dusting off of her skin, their use done so the magick holding them left.

I moved quickly, reaching for the dazed and injured weres and witches. I slammed my hands against them, putting teleporting jumps on their fronts and backs. They stumbled around, some crying as if they didn't even realize I was there. I couldn't blame them, that sound was loud enough even my own ears were ringing slightly and I was blocked from it. I tagged as many as I could before they started to regroup. I stood on the stairs and held my hands out, grinning as all eyes turned to me.

I clenched my fists, activating the jumps and as I put one on each person's chest and back they were torn to pieces instantly, blood spraying into the air as body parts flung rapidly in every direction. Shock made the air seem still and I laughed loudly at the display.

That was better than exploding people.

I didn't allow them to regroup as I sent a bolt of pure energy towards a witch, blowing her head off and sending her body flying at a couple of burned weres.

I glanced around and realized my werewolf was still MIA. "Ren, if you don't beast up I will start thinking you have performance anxiety." A snarl was the only response I got and I shoved over a charred witch, laughing as she fell into pieces as he hit the stairs. I glanced over and Ren's beasty finally showed up, grasping the edge of the altar and launching upwards, diving towards two weres with a roar of rage. "Much better!" I jerked to the side as my magick warned me of an incoming impact and a clay gollum let out a roar as its tree like club slammed in the spot I had just occupied.

I had forgotten about that asshole.

I scowled before sending a line of flames from my hand, encasing the clay creature, baking the clay of his body so he was unable to move. I narrowed my eyes before looking for the witch who teleported him behind me. I sensed her magick by one of the side pillars and I held my hand out towards the gollum before clenching my hand. His body shattered and I whipped my hand towards where she was, sharp sharps of fire hardened pottery flung towards her.

I enjoyed her screams as she tried to escape but were cut short as the pieces flew through her body, killing her. I continued up the stairs. "I'll be right there, beauty!" I sang the words to her as I glanced up at her, beaming as I pushed another charred body down the stairs. She smiled back at me, giggling again. I could hear Ren tearing into his opponents and I skipped across the large stairs, feeling the witches as they regrouped. "Oh laaaaadiiiieeess!" I sung the last word, grinning widely as my magick flared through me.

"You fucking, bitch! Do you know what you have done?" The words were spat out as a witch encased in a blue force field stepped into view, she walked towards me, her magick crackling in the air as her shield continually hummed its magick. I made a face as her before turning sideways, getting into a batter's position.

"I did as you should have and told these assholes no." I felt my magick solidify in my hands and I watched her approach before I swung my magick at here with all my might. The force of my swing made my magick connect with her shield with a resonating boom before it launched her into the air and over the trees. I put my hands on my hips and grinned as I watched her fly into the night sky.

I was shoved hard from behind and I hit the stairs with a heavy oof as a huge body landed on top of me, the scent of a magick bolt passing over top of us. I gave a sharp noise of agitation before the weight was gone and the beast who tackled me headed towards where the witches were.

I rolled my eyes before getting up and dusting myself off, in an exaggerated fashion. "A little warning would have been nice!" I called it out after Ren and was soon distracted by the sound of a heavy growl.

I turned and a hulking were looked down at me. I blinked up at him before grinning as I looked him up and down. "Aren't you a fine specimen." He came closer and I reached out and grabbed his junk, squeezing it as I put a moving portal on his junk. He doubled over as I squeezed harder, tilting my head as I gave a playful pout. "Not big enough for me. Sorry." I let his happy toys go and he hit his knees, cupping at his package with a pained sound.

I flounced off, looking for my next target and a witch came flying out from her hiding spot with a scream before she hit the stairs hard. Ren's snarls and snaps let me know he probably tossed her. She scrambled to her feet and froze when she saw me. I blinked at her and she whirled around, going to run off before I reached out and smacked her ass, putting a moving portal on her as I did so.

"I think he is big enough for you!" I watched as she ran down the stairs and grinned before clenching my hand, watching the werewolf zip down the stairs with his junk leading the way. I chortled with heavy amusement as his junk struck her ass with enough force to send her face first into the stairs, her bones snapping as he landed on top of her. Both of them tumbled down the stairs hard, their bones snapping and their cries of pain growing louder and louder.

I smirked before running up the stairs. I could feel more people coming, could feel the magick of a large portal opening up. All of my amusement faded as I reached Bo. I shoved the charred warlocks out of the way as I snapped my fingers, my magick unlocking the manacles that kept Bo into place.

She ran for me and I picked her up. "*Ren!*" He needed to get her out. I couldn't protect her or him with the fighting forced getting bigger. The werewolf I needed bolted from where ever he had been, his form coated in blood. He lifted his chin and I could feel the portal start to open up behind me and I tossed Bo towards him. "You need to get out!" He caught her quickly and looked at me right as the portal ripped open, magick surging through it as the reinforcements arrived.

He didn't move and I narrowed my eyes. "Go!" I shot out my hand and a long line of flame raced towards him, forcing him to bolt.

I whirled around, grinning at the witches and weres that came through as I held out my hands from my sides, my magick building and growing within me. "Come on!" I laughed as I shot first and took off a witch's head. "Let's fucking *dance*!" They paused for a fraction of a moment, watching her body crumple before they immediately whirled around and attacked.

Chapter Nineteen
Debt Owed

Run

My instinct surged through me, increasing my speed as I held Bo to my chest tightly. There was an intense feeling of relief having her safe in my arms. I had been sparred the only punishment that could break our species. Confusion warred with anger within me. I didn't know what to think anymore, who to trust. The witchling had betrayed us and then attacked those she had betrayed us to. She made no sense and I could see the slight madness hidden within her. It gleamed in her eyes as she stood bathed in moonlight and fire.

Ruuuunnn

My instinct shoved at me, the sounds of explosions, snarling, and screams following us through the trees. The battle still raged, still pushed onwards, the small witchling against an army. I didn't know whether to want her to die in the battle or to survive it so I could kill her myself. I darted around trees, leaving the sounds of the fighting behind us. Bo clung to me, uncaring of the smell of death, ash, and blood that clung to my skin. She looked around with curiosity at the trees as they blurred passed.

I skidded to a stop, the sounds had faded enough for me to make a stand. I leapt at a tree, my claws digging into the bark as I swung upwards, keeping Bo kept close to my chest. I climbed further into the tree before depositing Bo onto a branch. She wrapped her arms around the tree trunk and nodded at me and I dropped to the ground, scanning the trees, listening for approaching footsteps.

If I strained my hearing I could faintly hear the sounds of battle, the explosions from magick hitting magick faintly rocking the night as piercing screams echoed into the dark. The witching moon watched it all from her place in the sky. I wondered if she enjoyed the violence as much as the betraying witchling did. I could remember her joy, her runes flashing pink and amber on her skin as she decimated her enemies with a mere wave of her hand. Blood and viscera had followed in her wake.

Be wary

My instinct slowly wrapped around me, tightening my stomach as I barred my teeth, slowly pacing back and forth, inhaling deep lungfuls of the night air as the sounds faded to nothing. The silence was even more eerie than the sounds of death. I crouched down, staying close to the tree but slowly creeping through the shadows, my eyes darting around, looking for anything that would come for me and Bo.

The silence became heavier as time dragged on. The Forest was still and silent, it waited for action with a bated breath. Everything had been spooked by the battle, their calls silencing for fear of being destroyed as well. I narrowed my eyes, moving around trees, watching the moon and the forest itself.

Listen

My instinct rasped the word into my ear and I stilled my movements, tuning my hearing, straining it to hear what was needed. A faint curse entered my ear from far off and I bared my teeth with anticipation. Someone approached and they would die.

Get ready

The sound of sticks cracking underneath feet started growing clearer and there was an angry muttering that was carried in on the breeze. I inhaled deeply but could smell nothing but ash, magick, and blood. I shifted, silently moving through the brush, trying to find the right place to ambush my prey. I listened to see if there were more than one but no other voice joined the agitated murmuring.

It grew louder and louder and my heart pumped in my chest as the adrenaline of the hunt soared through my veins. I still, waiting for the perfect opportunity to attack when I faltered. The witch stumbled from the dark, her skin glowing and smoke rising over her. She moved as if dazed, shaking her head and muttering words I couldn't hear under her breath. Her clothing was scorched and nearly missing and I could see burn marks on the exposed parts of her flesh.

Anger punched my stomach hard and fast and I launched at her, pinning her to the ground, my hand around her throat with an angry snarl. She had betrayed me and Bo and I wanted to wring the life from her pretty little body.

"Kill you!" I tightened my grip just a fraction and the witch stared up at me before laughing, the sound vibrating her throat underneath her palm. I bared my teeth, squeezing tighter until the sound was choked off. "Owe me." The words were straggled as they came from her throat but she did nothing to get me to loosen my grip. She didn't move, didn't attempt to push me away. I didn't understand her.

I snarled at her words. "Betrayed us!" I wanted to crush her beneath my hands, wanted to coat my teeth with her blood and feast on her poisonous flesh. I had grown close with her, had trusted her, and she betrayed me.

She gave another straggled laugh that I cut off with a squeeze of my hand. "Did I?" The words were rasped and I could hear her body wiggling underneath me as she wheezed for air. Her emerald green eyes were amused as she looked up at me. "Oops." I snarled at her. I wanted to crush her but I couldn't, no matter how hard I strained to do just that my hand refused to close, to cut off her oxygen completely.

"Why?!" I roared the word at her and she smirked, her eyes taunting me with her mirth. She was *amused* by my anger. The witchling was mad! Insanity coursed through her veins if she thought taunting a rage filed were was a good idea.

I leapt off of her, tugging at my hair as I stared at her. I wanted to kill her, wanted to hurt her, but her reactions were confusing me. My head hurt because of what she was doing, how she was acting.

She lifted herself up, rubbing at her throat as she looked at me. "Kinky, were." A sinful smirk crossed her mouth and I shook my head as I looked at her raking her eyes down my form. "Remind me to remind you that next time we have sex if you want to choke me I am *all* for it." She winked at me and I shook harder.

"Insanity. Pure insanity." It was all that I knew, the witchling was insane. The urge to destroy her was deep within my gut but she showed no fear, no terror. She was twisting my mind with her reactions to my treatment. Anyone else would have been in tears, would have pissed themselves with my hand around their throat and she had *laughed.*

She shifted so she was leaning back on her elbows, giving her head a shake, making fly away curls from her braid sway around her ethereal face. "Only on the odd days." She grinned at me and I snapped my teeth, my agitation hitting me hard and fast.

"You taunt me!" She defied me, taunted me, again and again. She had no self preservation! "Want to *kill* you!" I thumped my fist against my chest hard. I wanted my body to listen. I wanted to fulfill the urge I had to take her flesh with my teeth.

"Then why don't you? I'm right here, fresh from a fight, and just about tapped out. You won't have a better chance." She looked at me, gesturing down her body as she crossed her ankles, tilting her head as she stared at me. "You can't can you?" A smirk tugged up her lips and I snarled, starting my pacing, back and forth, my muscles tense from the aggression that raced through me.

"Doesn't matter to me but I do know you have to suck up *hardcore.*" She grinned at me with that and I gave a heavy growl, stalking towards her.

"Betrayed *me!*" I stopped by her feet, looming over her. "Owe *me!*" I thumped my chest again. She had told them where we were, had betrayed Bo and I. Had allowed Bo to be captured and taken, to be nearly defiled. My anger surged up hard and fast once more, my hands aching to be wrapped around her pale throat but I couldn't reach out and grab her.

"I gave up being queen and living in a wicked awesome castle with hundreds of servants to slum it in the woods with you. You owe me. *Big*." She uncrossed her ankles and pulled her knees up before blatantly looking me up and down, her eyes finally landing on my cock that twitched under neath her intense gaze. "I demand sex as my compensation." She slowly spread her knees, licking her lips lightly and my cock slowly hardened, it didn't care about betrayal. It only cared about a wet and willing female it could be buried deep into.

I hit my knees before I realized I had moved, my hand reaching out and grabbing the back of her head, tugging her close. "Never trust you." I would never trust her again. I would leave with Bo, leave the witchling alone for what she had done.

Chapter Twenty
Rule Breaker

I stared at the werewolf who loomed over me but I felt no danger from him, a sense of comfort and security despite the anger in his eyes that begged to destroy me. I had betrayed him but I had my reasons. "He kidnapped me, Ren." I said the words slowly. I had never felt more violated than I had in that stupid King's bedroom. "He had me stripped and left me exposed for his viewing as if I was nothing but a pretty doll he could play with." I ground my teeth together. His eyes on me brought me no pleasure, it brought me wariness and hate. I didn't like that *arrogant fucking male.* He had played games with my life and violated the consent of my body. I didn't even respect him!

Ren looked at me and his eyes flashed yellow and gleamed. There was a part of him that wanted to trust me. I knew there was. I just needed to make it grow as his hand fisted at the back of my head, capturing my hair tightly as he pulled me a fraction closer, letting me feel his breath against my skin. I shivered under it, never letting my eyes drop from him.

"He took me to the balcony, sung a pretty song of lies and offered me a deal I never intended to take." I never wanted that fucking warlock! And it *burned* me to have to play like I did.

Ren snarled at me, his face growing more angular. "But you did!"

"Did I?" I snapped the words out. "I was in nothing but skimpy lingerie, next to the King of the fucking Covens, who had me on a balcony over looking a very long fall." I wasn't fucking stupid. The King hadn't been giving me the option of a no. My no would have had me tossed over the edge. I might have survived but then I would have been taken to the dungeons. "I did what I had to, to make it back to you!" I wouldn't be questioned on what I did. Everything I did was to make sure I made it back to protect the stupid idiot in front of me.

"So when he told me he would give me anything to have me cooperate, I asked him if I could kill you after it was done. And the stupid fucking idiot bought it." I narrowed my eyes at the werewolf. "It brought me right to the altar, right next to you, and to Bo. And it gathered all the fucking assholes into one place so I could fucking *kill them all.*" No one took what I wanted away from me and I wanted Ren and Bo. "Do you fucking get it, you dense piece of shit?" He let me go, leaning back as he looked at me through narrowed eyes.

I pulled myself to sitting as I glowered right back at him. "Currently, fuck you, you ungrateful bastard. I want my beauty." I stood up, walking away from him, seeking the little female out with my magick, feeling my spells still on her. I made a beeline right to her tree before I waved my hand, removing the spell I had placed on her to protect her ears. "Bo-peep?" I looked up and she jumped out of the tree, giggling as I caught her, spinning her around and peppering her face with relieved kisses. "You did *so* well!" I pressed my cheek to hers holding her tightly to my chest. She had played her part perfectly, doing just as I said.

A warm arm wrapped around me and Ren pushed his forehead against my temple, a rumbling in his chest as he pulled me closer. "Witchling stupid." He said the words low and rasping and my mouth dropped open.

"*Excuse me*? I'm a fucking genius!" Not just anyone could have crafted my plan in the span of ten minutes and have it be executed perfectly without any practice. "I played the King of the Covens like a two bit fiddle, I got everyone I absolutely hated into one area, and had the foresight to paint runes on Bo that triggered when the warlocks touched her, turning her into a fucking live grenade that killed a bunch of enemies." I sniffed, turning my head away from him as Bo giggled, nuzzling my cheek with her nose.

"Bam smart." At the two words I felt myself melt before pressing a kiss to her cheek.

"Thank you, lovey." I leaned my forehead against hers with a soft smile. "Let's go home." I pulled away and she nodded happily.

Ren let out a faint growl, shaking his head. "Cabin's destroyed." I slowly turned to look at him, my eyes narrowing.

"This *stupid* witch has a second cabin hidden away on a different dimensional plain because she is too paranoid to trust anyone." I sniffed at him before turning my head away. The asshole called me stupid. That was one way to get permanently cock blocked.

A rumble of a chuckle vibrated his chest as his grip tightened on me. "Smart witch." He nearly breathed the word into my ear and I narrowed my eyes. He knew me being upset wasn't conducive to getting him laid.

"Too late now. My feelings are hurt." I ignored him as he brushed his nose across my jawline, even though I shuddered under the feeling. I waved my hand, calling up the familiar portal to my interdimensional hide out. I watched it open up and glow around the edges. I headed for it but Ren's grip stopped me short.

I slowly turned to look at him, narrowing my eyes. "Hands off." I dared him to ignore me. "We've got to go." I gestured to the portal and flicked his arm off my waist before walking through the portal.

A warm and sweet air brushed over me as I landed on the plain that I had carefully created over the years I had been banished. I set Bo down, she seemed to handle the portal better than her last one. She giggled and took off right towards the tire swing hanging on the large oak tree. Ren's arms wrapped around me as I watched Bo jump onto the swing.

"They won't find us here." Locator spells wouldn't reach across the dimensions. No one could ever find us. We needed that because the fact I double crossed the King of the Covens while I had both birds high in the air meant I didn't have any more friends in the Covens.

"Still betrayed us." His voice was low and I could tell it was still bothering him. "Punish you later." He didn't need to specify for what as I felt him pressed against my ass.

"It's not punishment if I enjoy it." I smirked slightly at how he stiffened at my words before a rumble vibrated his chest. I knew anything he did to me I would enjoy. Even if I was miffed at him for calling me stupid. "As for the betrayal, you are safe now and most of those dicks are dead." I had taken out a few werewolves as well as numerous witches. I thought it was hilarious that Ren and I had single-handedly united the two species who had been segregated for more than six hundred years.

"Still hunt us." His voice was guttural and I nodded. They would and I would have to make sure Ren made it worth the target on the back of my head.

"Yup. I double crossed the Warlock King. That's a very large target painted on us." I made a face. The guy was attractive but pretty didn't cover asshole and that warlock was all sorts of asshole. I didn't doubt for a moment that he would have pitched me off the balcony if I had said no to him. "Stupid prick deserved it." I narrowed my eyes, watching Bo as she swung on the swung underneath the vastness of the stars.

"What he offer you?" The question was asked low and against my ear but I knew what he was referencing.

"Besides a castle and to be queen? He offered me a son." A sweet little boy that I ached to have in my arms. How I imagined what he had told me, a sweet cherubic little boy that called me mummy and gave me sticky kissed. "But he can't give me the son I want." I looked up at Ren, meeting his dark gaze. "Because I want a little boy who's eyes *gleam*."

Epilogue
Well Pleased

Feast

Dark whispers trailed around my spine as I watched her. Red hair like flames hallowed her pale, ethereal face. She was a bounty given to us. One we had enjoyed over and over again and my cock swelled and hardened to enjoy her once more.

Take what is given freely

Instinct demanded I take her like the beast I was, to bend her over and bury myself deep within her silky, clutching walls until she could do nothing but whimper my name again and again. I wanted to take her until she could barely make a sound, so lost in my possession that she had lost the ability to weave her spells around me. I wanted her limp and blissful as I branded my claim into her body. There were many before me but I wanted her to remember none but me.

Feast, the bounty is there

She moved across the small room, her hips swayed sensually from side to side. Her emerald green eyes watched me like a lazy cat would. I bared my teeth as she crawled onto the bed, her lips curling into a smirk as she straddled my waist. I gave a low growl as she brushed my cock with her ass. She made a throaty sound of amusement that I narrowed my eyes at. She taunted the wrong beast.

"Such a night, my little beasty." Her hands spread across my chest, my muscles bunching as I bared my teeth and grabbed her hips with a growl. That small sound of amusement turned into a throaty chuckle that sent blood rushing straight to my cock. She was a temptress, always teasing and testing until she got what she wanted. Me buried deep inside of her wet heat. "Apologies, my *not* so little beasty." She reached behind her and I gave a deep groan as she grasped my length. I bucked into her grasp but she gave another amused chuckle and let go.

"Those horrid creatures are dead and our little beauty is sound asleep." She sat up straighter and toyed with the hem of the shirt she was wearing. I knew it was one of mine and I liked seeing her wrapped up in it. I liked seeing her stiff nipples brushing against the fabric through her thin bra and my instinct drove me to bite them. To tease them until she begged me and then plunge my cock deep inside of her until she screamed for me. "I wonder what we could do with our time." Her voice trailed off as she gave me a wicked smile that had my blood roaring through my veins.

I attempted to lift her off of me to throw her onto the bed but she shoved my hands away and rocked back and forth on my stomach with a languid grin. "We have a problem, my big ol' beast man." She sucked her bottom lip into her mouth and I gave a deep growl of discontent. My instinct to breed the female would not be denied. "You see... witches are a very... *monogamous* breed." Her slashing green eyes narrowed as she waved her hand slowly at the wall and the lights dimmed. Magick crackled against my skin so lightly it was almost non-existent.

"This causes me a very big issue with you." She rocked backwards and caught the head of my cock underneath her generous ass and I breathed heavily through my nose, glaring up at her as my instinct roared at me.

Breed

She brought her finger to her lips and tapped it slowly, drawing my gaze from her eyes to the plumpness that begged to be wrapped around my shaft as I fed it deep into her throat. "You see... I want to be with you, Ren. However, your instinct will demand you run off if my fields do not produce from your generous seed." She tsked softly and I narrowed my eyes at her words. She wasn't wrong. Even now my instinct demanded a frenzy of mating but I could smell her infertility. Her inability to produce with the seed I had given. I would leave her. It was a matter of time.

"You would leave and take my munchkin with you. That does not sit well with me because I am getting rather attached to her and well..." She bit her lip and her eyes went hooded as she slid backwards and my cock rubbed against the silky fabric coating the heat that I wanted to bury myself into. "I am getting *very* attached to this." She rocked her hips, touching her neck and cupping her breasts as her eyes fluttered from the pleasure she was obviously getting.

My chest rumbled as I caught scent of her readiness. I could shove her onto her back and I would find her sopping for me. Her body demanding its due from me. It *craved* my seed. My instinct roared at me.

Ignore her words
Breed her

"I want you to stay, Ren, but I know you will leave me and make me share you with other females." Her full bottom lip stuck out in a pout and she gaze down at me with an almost hurt expression. "But perhaps..." The pout faded as she pulled the shirt up her pale legs, baring her spread thighs for me. My mouth dried and my instinct hammered at my skull as the scrap of fabric she passed for underwear was revealed.

How I loved seeing her bent over with it running up between the two globes of flesh she had for an ass. She drew the shirt up and off and my eyes devoured the banquet for flesh she had uncovered for me. Her tits were pushed up in that thin lace contraption that I wanted to pull off with my teeth so I could nip at that silky flesh. My cock stiffened further and my instinct started its crawl down my spin as it hissed at me.

Take her now
Wet and willing
She will welcome it deep

My hands itched and claws pushed out of my nail beds. I wanted her on her back as I drove into her hard. I wanted her to squeal and cum around me as I punished her for her current torment. I stared at the pale flesh she revealed before poison green runes were illuminated high up on her right thigh. They glowed against her pale skin and they wrapped around her thigh almost to her knee. My instinct recoiled and I bared my teeth at it aggressively. I didn't want that on her skin. My instinct hissed words I couldn't hear as I stared at the markings on her skin.

"I could take this off." The runes slid across her skin wrapping around her thigh as they were drawn to her hand. They swirled in the air above her palm, the poisoned green glow illuminating her flesh in a sickly colour. "You see this is a very strong spell. It was cast a very long time ago and we get it placed on us as infants." Her green eyes glowed almost cat like and the instinct hissed and snarled at the magick that swirled above her palm. It was not a good spell.

"Normally the only people who can remove it would be an Elder witch on my wedding day to my warlock husband but those are in short supply and I'm far too good to be trapped by any spell. I learned how to get rid of it ages ago but I kept it. It was very useful for me." She stared at the spell swirling in her palm before a chilling smile crossed her face. "This spell is special. Created specifically with werewolves in mind." She swirled her palm and those glowing green runes danced above her palm. She seemed almost mesmerized by them.

I grabbed her hips with a deep rumbling in my chest. I wanted her to stop playing with the foul magick she had in her hand. There was nothing but empty death within the runes.

"So impatient, Ren." She rolled her eyes as she looked at me, her green eyes glowing with the magick she was using. "You see. Witches are very fertile. So fertile in fact that without this little spell, if you came right here." She tapped her finger below her belly button and I gave a deep groan at the thought of my seed smeared across her pale skin. I wanted that, *needed* that. "I would still probably get knocked up." She gave me a wide cat like grin as if she had loved the very thought. I brushed the words away, she smelled incompatible with me and scents did not lie. I would enjoy her while my instinct allowed.

"So... I know your instinct will demand you leave me if I don't give it what it wants. There is only so much amazing pussy will do to calm that beast underneath your skin." She let out a heavy sigh and I ground my teeth together, rocking my hips up. Amazing pussy, mind blowing pussy that I wanted to be buried in up to my aching balls. "And it *is* amazing pussy but even it has its limitations. I can't fault it for that." She blew an errant red curl away from her face as she wiggled her fingers lazily, the spell dancing in the air, swirling around and around., their glow flickering slightly.

Foul spell
Beware of magick
It brings death

I ground my teeth together as she looked down at me. That spell had to go or I needed to leave. It was making me agitated and more and more aggressive as my instinct slithered through my veins. She shifted above me and my thoughts blanked as I let out a pained groan. Despite the instinct's agitation, my cock was still hard for her.

"My problem is that if I remove this handy bit of magical contraception, I can't put it back on. So that means if you fuck off on me, any male can come along and impregnate me." She looked perturbed at the thought and the instinct seized in rage.

My female
Mine to use

No others

The rumbling in my chest grew harsher as my teeth filled my mouth. She would not be taken by another male while within my reach.

"Didn't like that?" She stared down at me as her face turned stony. "Just like I don't like the thought of you traipsing through this world sticking your cock into other females after we made a deal. I wouldn't be nice, Ren. If I caught a whiff of you with another woman. I would wait until you were buried balls deep into her snatch and then chop your fucking cock off. Then I would shove it down her throat. Give her enough of your cock until she choked and died from it." Her blunt teeth bared at me in aggression as several other spells on her skin glowed an angry amber.

Good female

My instinct purred the words at me and I grinned at her, baring all my sharply pointed teeth back at her. She was such a brutal female. She was not a simpering werefemale or a cold and modest witch. She was brutal and wicked and I liked the female threatening me. I slid my grips down to her thighs and squeezed hard as my cock throbbed almost painfully. She was teasing me again.

"I don't like sharing." The words came out clipped and angry, showing me her territorial aggression towards the imaginary females. "If you agree to be with me, you will be with me until we both die or I will kill you." She scowled at me before her bottom lip slowly stuck out. "I don't want to kill you, Ren. I really like you." She crooned the words as she rocked her hips with a faint sound of pleasure low in her throat. I could feel her leaking on me through the thin fabric separating us.

Female ready

Take her now

Instinct was surging through me, getting me ready to throw her down as I ripped the fabric away from that hot little pussy of hers but one more swirling motion with her hand brought the glowing green spell back to our minds.

"So you have a choice, Ren. I can take this off and you and I can spend the rest of our happily miserable lives together with our little munchkin and all the other little munchkins you want. Or you can fucking leave now. I won't waste my time on an ungrateful male." She stared down at me and I narrowed my eyes as I bared my teeth at her.

"Blackmail?" Deny me sex for a future? It sounded like blackmail. My instinct hissed at that and the urge to dominate her, to punish her was thick within me.

"*Negotiations.* You can be with me forever or you won't be with me at all." She lifted her head up, her curls brushing the tops of her breasts. The glowing green the runes let off made her seem more witchy and strangely more alluring. A woman with a poisoned apple in her hand as she offered to give me a bite. "I need an answer." A demanding female. She needed to be put in her place. I gave a heavy snarl as I sat up, my hands clutching her tightly as I ground into her. I wouldn't give her up until my instinct demanded it of me.

"Choose." Her hot breath brushed my skin and I buried my face into her neck before I trailed my teeth up her skin to her jaw. My instinct wasn't liking her scent. There was too much going on and it could scent our incompatibility for offspring. A few weeks with her or the rest of my life without her. My cock made the decision for me.

"I'll try with you, witchling." The words were guttural but not the promise she would have wanted. Demanding females wouldn't be given what they wanted.

"Good." Her mouth slipped across my skin as she shoved me back onto the bed and bent down, her lips brushing my ear. The spell was otherworldly as it escaped her mouth and magick sparked across my skin as her words travelled through the air. She sat up and showed me the palm with the green runes swirling above it. I watched as they slowly blackened, crumbling as if they were rapidly burned without evident fire. They turned to ash and disappeared entirely. "Keep me happy, wolfman. You know what I do to those who displease." Her eyes flashed with demanding.

My instinct seethed to life, the magick that pushed it away was gone and it could return to full force. I threw her off of me and forced myself between her thighs as she bounced on her back. A deep growl filled the air as I tore at the flimsy underwear that kept me from her core. My nostrils flared as I took in her honeyed scent. I would keep her well pleased. She would want for nothing while the instinct drove me to continue to find purpose between her pale thighs.

Take female
Breed her
She is willing

Her knees spread for me, opening up her hot and ready core to my gaze. I salivated at the scent of her before I reached up and yanked her bra down below her breasts. They bounced with the movement and I descended on them, nipping and tonguing the flesh with a vengeance. I wanted her *writhing* for me.

Feast on the bounty
Feed on her flesh
Devour her honey
Plant your seed

I gave a heavy snarl as I clamped my teeth down on the top of her breath. She whined but her hands went over her head instead of trying to push me away. Her hips moved against the blankets in an unrelenting pattern, attempting to coax me from her breasts.

"More." It came out guttural against her skin as I let go of the bruising mark I had given her. I needed to consume more.

"Keep me happy." She groaned the words out as I marked a nipping trail down to where her body wept for me. She twisted on the covers, her body sweating enough that I wanted to taste every inch of her. She tasted of sinful sex and magick. My cock jerked at it and I gave a heavy growl as I brought my face down to that pretty little sex she had hidden from me. I inhaled deeply and my instinct jerked to a stop as she gave a low and throaty chuckle.

Ferrrrtiiiiiiiiile

It was a rasping hiss like wind blown sand against my skin. I inhaled deeper, pushing in closer to her glistening folds as my eyes nearly rolled into the back of my head.

Fertile
Accepting
Compatible

With the foul spell gone from her flesh I could finally scent her and it was more than mouthwatering. It was nearly enraging as my cock tensed and seized with the need to be buried deep within her, to give her body what it was so carelessly demanding.

"I want a big family." The words were gasped as I drove my tongue into her, tasting her with a deep groan as I reached down and gave my pained shaft a hard tug. It would soon be buried within her. "I want to be pleased." My instinct raked down my spine harder than before. I had a willing and fertile female spread out before me and I needed to take her before another male attempted. Her words fluttered back into my mind. Another male could have her if I didn't take her.

Claim her
Sink deep

I lifted my head before I wrapped my arms around her thighs and yanked her down the covers so that she was spread out over my thighs. My shaft lay across her scorching wetness and I stared down at her intently, breathing heavily with my restraint. "What would please you?" The words were garbled and growled but her emerald green eyes shone up at me.

"Children." Her tone was soft as she looked up at me, her body slowly submitting to my own presence. I wanted to howl my victory as I watched the powerful witchling melt underneath me. "I wanna be barefoot and pregnant. Make it so." It was a faint demand with glistening eyes that begged me.

I thrust deep and her back bowed as her slick walls shuddered around my cock, clutching and pulsating as she came around me. I bared my teeth as I pulled back and roughly thrust again. She gave a choked cry as she twisted on the blankets.

Claim her
Mark her
Possess her
Breed her

I thrust into her aggressively, allowing her no respite from my brutal movements. She whimpered and moaned, her pert mouth begging me as I roughly took her. There seemed to be no end in the pulsating and contracting of her slick pussy. I scored her skin with my claws in satisfaction that I was drawing the pleasure out of her so brutally as I took her hard. I would erase any male before me and once my pup was in her belly, there would be none after me. My instinct would never allow me to walk away from her, from my pup. She would be claimed by me entirely. Mind, body, and soul.

I let out a heavy snarl as she once again came around me. My cock ached and I pulled out abruptly, flipping her onto her stomach before I shoved back in. I needed to take her like this. The instinct crawled up my spine, urging me to move faster, work her harder. She was mewling at me as her orgasms crashed over her without end. There would be no male that would ever turn her head after this claiming.

My balls tightened, letting me know I was close. I bent forward as my hips moved faster, pistoning into her as I dug my teeth into her shoulder tightly. The sound of flesh smacking flesh filled the air and she came around me wetly, drenching me as she stiffened and shuddered with a keening cry escaping her throat. I gave a grunt and unleashed my seed deep into her, thrusting as far as I could into her before I pulled back and thrust again. I unleashed my instinct's need to claim her fertile ground deep within her as she shuddered beneath me. Again and again I seared her needing body with what it wanted.

I slowed to a stop still buried deep within her. I pulled my teeth from her shoulder as I straightened up. There was no softening to my cock as I pulled back and drove into her again. A puff of air escaped her as her arms collapsed and she pressed her face into the covers. I reached forward and buried my hand into her red curls and pulled back, lifting her face up out of the blankets.

"Take it all." I growled it out to her as my hips hit that perfect ass of hers and my instinct howled its satisfaction in its claiming. She wouldn't be released until I was finished. I gave a feral grin as she gave a sharp cry that signalled another orgasm crashing over her.

My female would be *well* pleased.

Author's Note

Thank you for reading my first instalment of Twisted Dark!

This is part one of a novella series that I wrote on a whim. It turned into so much more than I had first thought and it has developed into a five book novella series.

It is a *drastic* change from my previous books. It's naught and sexy and completely out there but I loved writing it! I had great fun with BamBam as a character and just going out there and creating her was something I hadn't imagined I was capable of. She was crazy confident, sexually empowered and 100% insane.

I hope you guys loved reading this novella just as much as I did writing it.

Until next time
Anna M. L. Koski

Acknowledgements

I need to acknowledge those who helped me through this process once more. This time *was* easier than the first one but that doesn't mean that the support and love I received wasn't appreciated or wanted. It truly was and I want to thank everyone from the bottom of my heart.

I would firstly like to thank my mum. She has always been there for me and believed in me every step of the way. She has never once faltered in her guidance and love for me and that is something I doubt there will be words I can every express to encompass how much I love her for it.

I would also like to thank my sister, for whom the book is dedicated. They once again have been a *very* great support system for me. I cannot express ho much I love them and how much each of them mean to me.

I would also love to once again thank my readership and community for their unfailing support and appreciation in all that I do in my writing. They are always full of encouragement and happiness and never once let me fall. They have always been there for me and they have never been anything but loving and supportive.

And of course my last thank you. This is once again to my best friend and twinsie, Ashley. Once again she is my second half, and there is nothing that can encompass how much I love her for being by my side through my crazy episodes with my anxiety or bouts of stress I endured while writing my stories. She is and always will be like a sister to me no matter where life takes us. So once again, I love you and thank you for being there for me.

About the Author

Anna M. L. Koski grew up on the family homestead in the rolling hills of Southern Saskatchewan. She has always been an avid writer and has a boundless love of literature.

Time has not lessened her desire to write but has only seemed to make her passion for it that much stronger as the years have gone by. You will likely find her staring at her laptop writing page after page of her stories even in the wee hours in the morning.

She has a great love of encouraging others to follow their dreams and to pursue their passions. She believes a life is only well lived if it is lived in happiness and contentment. She lives by her mother's motto and encourages others to do the same.

The tallest trees have the strongest roots.
Never forget where you came from.

Coming Soon

Shadow of the Beast

Twisted Dark

Anna M.L. Koski

Introducing the Second book in the Twisted Dark Series!
Shadow of the Beast

Read further for sneak peek of the newest instalment!

Violet has never belonged to herself.

She has been under the thumb of a cruel Elder Irma since she was born, stuck looking at the world and never being allowed to experience it. Her magick is bound tightly within her and with a chain around her ankle, she is trapped.

It all changes when a massive werewolf named, Jax, nearly destroys the shop and kidnaps her in his search of Irma. Yanked away from everything she knows, she's suddenly in the world she's never been able to touch with nothing but a dangerous werewolf to rely on.

Jax wants nothing but his brother but he soon sets his eyes on Violet, interest making them gleam. She's stuck between trusting him, her desire, and the world that threatens to destroy them both if she falls to the northern werewolf's charm.

However, without magick and no way to help Jax find Irma, she knows that the chain will forever remain around her ankle and she will continually be at the whims of those who hold the end of it. Be it a cruel witch or a rugged werewolf.

Clink Clack
Take your freedom back

Chapter One
Gold Coins

"One thousand eight hundred and thirty-three." I sighed out the number, setting my last gold coin on its stack. The brilliant yellow of the gold coins always made me feel better and if I needed to feel better it was now. I still hadn't quite recovered from Florence's... *visit.* A phantom pain ran over my nerves and I shivered at the memory of claws slowly moving through my flesh as the vicious witch had asked me the same questions again and again.

Where were the two werewolves? '*What werewolves?*' hadn't been acceptable.

Who were they with? '*I don't know.*' hadn't been acceptable.

Do you know where they went? '*I don't understand.*' hadn't been acceptable either.

It took me three long and drawn out deaths before I had finally cracked. I blinked back tears at that. I cursed the very day I was born and handed off to the brutality of Elder Irma. I shifted my left foot, the thin chain locked around my ankle forever reminding me of my position. I had no clue how Florence had learned of the time check spell on the chain and I had a sneaking suspicion it had been Irma who had told her.

I wasn't a fucking idiot, the very last witch I wanted to piss off was Miranda Lenkirion but I could only take being killed and regenerated so many times before my fear of it happening again overrode my fear of the powerful witch. The fucking time check *curse* on my chain meant that I could be killed but I wouldn't stay dead. I would be back in the land of the living when the time check spell lost my pulse. It reversed the damage and brought me back to the point of when the spell was last activated and it was activated daily.

It was like I was stuck in a form of hellish stasis. Dying was a *horrible* thing to endure and I had endured it a lot. It was why the gold was so comforting to me. I was trying to get enough gold to buy my freedom from Elder Irma. I had no clue what the debt I owed was but gold was hard to come by and I had gotten a significant amount of it. Nearly two thousand coins was a very generous amount and it was hard earned. I had to deal with illegal potions out of the back door of the shop to gather my gold. Elder Irma didn't pay me, slaves didn't get paid.

I shoved the thought away. I *would* pay for my freedom and I *would* be free of the chain on my ankle. I just needed to sell a few more potions and I would have over two thousand gold coins. I knew that Elder Irma would have a hard time refusing that size of payment. I just hoped it was tempting enough for her to accept it and let me go.

I took care of the shop for her but since I had grown up she hadn't used me for her experiments. I was thankful for that, very thankful for that, but I just wanted to be free.

I let out a small sigh as picked up my coin bag, slowly putting stacks of coins into it. I hadn't been allowed to practice my magick, hadn't been allowed to test for my levels. I had looked at the world around me through a cage my entire life. I just wanted to experience *something* without a chain rubbing my ankle raw.

I managed to clear the table of my coins and I closed the bag, trying it shut. It felt a bit heavier and I could hear the coins clinking around in the velvet. It had an ever space spell on it. I could put as much stuff as I wanted into and it wouldn't weigh too much or become full. I had managed to get it as a trade for a wellness potion I had created that created the illusion of youth and vitality. It was time and effort well spent in my opinion.

I stood up from my spot at the back table before I walked towards my corner I did my best to ignore the faint sound of the tiny chain moving along the floorboards behind me. It just reminded me of my place, as did my corner. A tiny, lumpy mattress on a rope bed frame ticked between several barrels was where I called home. I knelt down and shoved at one of the wooden boards of the barrel closest to my bed. The piece shifted inwards and I wiggled the bag into place before pushing against the metal band of the barrel, popping the panel back into place.

I stood up, brushing my dusty hands off on my light dress. I knew I was being overly paranoid because Elder Irma never came around but I still didn't want to take any chances on anyone finding it. It paid to be paranoid, I knew that very well. I could hear the chime of the bell as the front door to the shop opened and I moved towards the warped mirror that stood over a rusty water basin and I smoothed down my hair, forcing a smile onto my face. There was no need for anyone to tell the Elder witch I wasn't being nice. She didn't come around but I also knew the witch never passed up on an opportunity to punish me.

I moved towards the front of the store, leaving the back quickly. The chain around my ankle became lighter and harder to see at the presence of another person around. Another little perk of the fucking chain, no one really knew it was there and I couldn't say anything about it or why I had it. Elder Irma didn't particularly like sharing and I knew that she knew that the spells on the chain made me a very special case if someone wanted to use me to get at her. That was probably also why I had no clue where Coven Thirteen was. The Elder witch was paranoid to a fault.

I tucked my hair behind my ears and once again pasted the smile on my face as I came around the front desk. "Welcome to the Broken Crow. How may I help you?" My voice trailed off as I blinked at the large form that nearly took up the entire doorway. I slowly looked up, my eyes following up the chest to a thick neck, that held several tattoos and a strong jaw and severely set mouth.

A glint of gold caught my attention as I spotted several small hoops rested along the male's ear lobe. My throat grew dry as I finally met the male's gaze. His eyes were a rather startling blue as they looked around the shop and his lips curled up into what looked like a snarl and his white teeth glinted against his tanned skin. The apparent and rather dangerous aura that hung off of him had my eyes widening and my heart racing with fear even before his eyes gleamed with a hint of ferality and a growl rumbled his chest.

A fucking *werewolf*.

I felt like my heart would escape my chest as I looked at the dangerous creature that had just decided to drop in. The last two times a werewolf had been in my shop something very bad had happened to me and I didn't think this time would be third time's the charm.

203

204

This book recognizes the upset this publishing has caused in certain individuals in a certain group but the author of this book does not care about the upset and those individuals can suck it.

Suck it.

CPSIA information can be obtained
at www.ICGtesting.com
Printed in the USA
BVHW061710020320
573817BV00009B/65/J